D1148936

ADVANTAGES OF
THE OLDER MAN

ADVANTAGES OF THE OLDER MAN

by

Gwyneth Lewis

SEREN

Seren is the book imprint of
Poetry Wales Press Ltd
57 Nolton Street, Bridgend, Wales, CF31 3AE
www.serenbooks.com
Facebook: facebook.com/SerenBooks
Twitter: @SerenBooks

ISBN: 978-1-78172-190-2
kindle: 978-1-78172-191-9
ebook: 978-1-78172-192-6

Typesetting by Elaine Sharples
Printed by CPI Group (UK) Ltd, Croydon

The publisher works with the financial assistance of
The Welsh Books Council

1

I know exactly the moment when the spirit of Dylan Thomas possessed me.

It was my restless hands. They've always got me into trouble, ever since I was a toddler and curiosity prompted me to stick my little finger into a pencil sharpener and turn it. Just to see what happened. The thing is, I did it not once, but twice.

Of course my parents were thrilled when I returned to Swansea after my time in London. They'd wanted me to come back as soon as I graduated from university but I held out for a job, my biggest rebellion in our relationship so far. I knew that once I went home my life would be over.

Not that London was glamorous. Sure, it sounded good, working in a gallery. But a community centre in Hackney was hardly Bloomsbury. Every night before going to bed, in the house I shared with an ever-changing succession of school teachers, swimming-pool attendants and the like, I'd lay out my breakfast dishes ready for the morning, covering the bowl with a paper serviette. I like being neat, prepared for everything. Some people have no respect for food which is clearly labelled in the fridge. How mean do you have to be to steal stewed pears from a Tupperware container clearly marked JENNIFER?

I never told my parents that I'd lost my virginity, although I felt so different on my first weekend home that I was sure that my mother would be able to tell. Was it my imagination, or did she take an extra deep breath as she greeted me at the station, as if she detected an alien smell about my person? If she did, she chose to ignore it and the weekend took its usual course of silent meals, *The Two Ronnies* and walks along Mumbles pier.

My hopes for a relationship never came to anything. I didn't have the knack of getting men to ask me out, let alone the marriage business. How do women get males to propose? The only thing I managed to work out was that a drunken man will never look a gift horse in the mouth, if you get my meaning. I didn't mind that they seldom stayed for breakfast, even though I always set out two places before I went out on a Saturday evening and opened an extra tin of fruit to go with the Weetabix, just in case.

When I first saw the advert for the job in the Dylan Thomas Art Gallery, I thought little of it. Then, just before the closing date, I sent an application. To this day I don't really understand why. We'd all been force-fed Dylan Thomas, what with us being from Swansea. 'Do not go gentle into that good night' and all that. Of course, there was the inevitable school production of *Under Milk Wood*. Was I given the part of Miss Myfanwy Price who secretly fantasised that she was called Dolores? Or Gossamer Beynon? Or how about sexy Polly Garter? Like hell. No, Susannah James, with her long blonde hair and brown eyes was given that part, probably because of that sweet singing voice she had. It was Mrs Ogmore-Pritchard for me, the woman who was an obsessive-compulsive cleaner. I was only ten, but I felt that I understood her character. After all, I'd grown up watching Mam vacuum lines into the front-room carpet, so that it looked like a well-kept lawn when the vicar called. She made me a special mobcap to match my

Victorian nightdress and assured me that it was a sign of my maturity that I'd been given the chance to play an older woman. I decided to give it my all and played it straight. I said my climactic line – 'And tell the sun to wipe its feet' – with such venom that, for a second, the audience was stunned. Then there followed a roar of laughter. My face flushed with shame and my eyes filled with tears. Once I got off stage, I ran to the toilet to hide. That was the last time I took part in amateur dramatics. Whenever Dylan Thomas's name was mentioned in our house, my mother would sniff and pronounce 'Pig of a man'.

The truth is, I don't even like poetry. It seems to me to have something essentially shaming about it, like acne. Why grown men and women should cultivate a way of speaking which seems designed to put other people off them, I don't know. It's like being proud of knowing how to stuff ships into bottles or being an enthusiast of morris dancing.

Romantic comedy is more my thing. You know, *When Harry Met Sally* or, my all-time favourite, *Sleepless in Seattle*. Proper romance between man and woman. Everything works out all right in the end. I think I nearly wore out the tape, watching the last scene at the top of the Empire State Building in New York, when Meg Ryan goes to meet Tom Hanks. I'd kill to be able to visit there and have my own peak moment. I think mine passed years ago and nobody noticed. What a waste.

Once the letter offering me the job arrived, I had to tell my parents. Mam was appalled. 'I won't let you have anything to do with that dreadful man!' She hit the arm of the settee so hard that a small puff of dust rose from the upholstery. 'I remember...'

She stopped abruptly as we both realised what she'd said. Incredulous, I asked: 'You knew him?'

She blushed, making much of rearranging the antimacassar on the sofa's arm.

'I might have met him, once or twice.'

'What was he like?'

'Horrible. I told you, nothing but trouble.'

'What did he ever do to you?'

For the first time ever, I saw my mother speechless. Her lips grew thin and she jumped up, furious, and dashed out to the kitchen, from where she shouted: 'Look what you've made me do! That cake will be burnt to a crisp! It's all your fault. Why don't you get a proper job, instead of wasting your time with arty types?'

She didn't speak to me or my father for two days. But the *bara brith* she set on the table that night looked fine to me. When she finally decided to rejoin the human race, she stated categorically, 'You'll be coming home to live.' Thinking of my Saturday nights, I'd fancied a one-bedroom flat in the new marina development, but my mother's tone of voice was absolute. I just didn't have the stomach for a fight. So, soon after, I found myself lying on the pink candlewick bedspread of my childhood room, staring at a map of Middle Earth.

Although the gallery was named after Dylan Thomas, it had little to do with the poet. My job was clerically straightforward and much less busy than the centre in Hackney. I was to man reception, keep accounts and be a general administrative assistant. Our office was in modern premises near the marina, just round the corner from the Swansea Museum – 'a museum which belongs in a museum', according to Dylan.

One lunchtime, I wandered into the Dylan Thomas Centre which was in the same quarter of the city. The ground floor housed a permanent exhibition of the poet's life. There were glass cases with samples of manuscripts, black-and-white photographs of the curly-headed poet, cigarette dangling from his mouth. My favourite exhibit was a vial of yellow liquid, claiming to be sweat from the poet's brow. To me, it looked more like urine. As I leant over it for an even closer look, I felt someone behind me.

'Strange to think that somebody's life could be large enough to be sustaining a visitors' centre and a tearoom fifty years after he died, isn't it?'

I turned to see a young man with long hair, holding a small Moleskin notebook. He was close enough that I could smell him. I liked his odour. I much prefer a bit of sweat to the chemical tang of aftershave. I simpered in return. When he made to move, I roused myself to say: 'Hell of a poet though, wasn't he?'

'My favourite. Which of his poems do you like best?'

I racked my brains but failed to remember a title.

'The … late work, I think.'

The man agreed and began to quote enthusiastically from Thomas's last poem. By the time we'd reached a bronze cast of Dylan Thomas's death mask, I knew that his name was Peter and he was a poet. The head was huge, as if it belonged to a centaur. The boyish features had thickened up, consolidated into a wide stubby nose and thick lips. It was a face that showed self-abuse, a corrupted cherub.

Peter had startling hazel eyes, although his glasses took away from them.

'And you? Do you write?' he asked.

'Oh, you know, a bit,' I lied.

'I expect you're being modest.'

'No, actually, I'm not.'

'You women poets always lack confidence,' he insisted. 'You should come to the open mic I run here the last Friday of every month. It would give you some reading experience.'

I noted the date, made plans. I was even prepared to write some drivel, if it meant a chance of going to the pub with this dream in a denim shirt.

So, I had Dylan Thomas to thank for my introduction to Pete Hodson. Here was a man who could save me from home. Because he loved poetry, I realised that I had to love it too, in order to become close to him. I became a regular at the open mic evenings, made myself indispensible. I didn't mind taking the readers' names, making posters and placing ads in the local newsletters. As time went by, Peter even trusted me with opening up on nights when he was working late at his job, teaching in a local school. At one of the evenings, Peter announced that the group of poets had been invited to enter a float for the Swansea carnival parade. I volunteered to help at once. We agreed that we'd all dress up as characters in *Under Milk Wood*. Peter said he would be First Narrator which, if you ask me, was a little predictable, but then he was the founder of the Friday night readings. I decided to make him sit up and take notice of me as a woman. His jaw dropped when, on carnival day, I presented myself as Dylan Thomas's Muse. I'd swathed my not insubstantial body in flowing but subtly revealing Grecian robes. While being towed by an old Massey Ferguson tractor along the Mumbles front, I jumped into action, performing an Isadora Duncan dance with all the sexual wiles I could muster. I modelled my dance on a photograph of the young Caitlin Thomas dancing on a riverbank. My dance focused around Peter. On the precarious platform, I know my performance made an impression on him – and the watching crowds – but I could have done without the incident involving the *Saturday Night Fever* float, which collided with us. The jolt sent me flying off my podium and into the road. Still, despite the awkwardness and the screaming match between the drivers – I'd like to know what busybody felt they had to call the emergency services – I think I behaved with dignity on the whole and won everybody over with my willingness (after I'd rearranged my dress) to carry on with the show, despite a nasty injury to the head.

I don't know if it was embarrassment or awe but, after that, things were never the same between me and Peter. He never gave any sign of seeing me as anything other than an occasional assistant. In fact, he seemed not to notice me at all. Neither did the whole of the male population of Swansea. I wondered vaguely if I'd already had my ration of passion.

That was before the virtual Dylan. In the pub one night after a particularly downbeat monthly reading, I was sitting with Peter and Bernard Mitchell, a Swansea photographer who'd been taking shots of my beloved. Peter was gloomy and had finished the evening off by reading a poem of his own called 'Elegy'. Even I, his biggest fan, thought it was a right downer and was glad when we went to the pub. I didn't quite know what to say about the poem, so I held my tongue. Peter was taciturn. Something had happened to darken his world. I would have done anything to cheer him up.

I was sitting next to Bernard, a lovely unassuming man, in whose company I felt comfortable. I was secretly hoping that he'd let me have a print of Peter to hide in my bedroom but I didn't get a chance to ask. Peter bought Bernard a drink and, as he relaxed, Bernard let slip that, as a young man, he'd taken portraits of Thomas's circle of friends – known collectively as the Swansea Gang – in the years immediately after the poet's death. Using a Rollieflex T, he created striking black and white images of the local artists – Daniel Jones, poet Vernon Watkins and artists Fred Janes and Ceri Richards. I called Peter over to hear more, knowing that he'd be fascinated. He brought his pint and sat opposite us.

Bernard said he regretted that he never photographed Dylan himself. He had, though, thought about the idea of creating a 3D image of the poet. Suddenly I felt more excited than I had at any moment since I'd come back to Swansea.

'You mean it would be like seeing him read one of his own poems?' asked Peter.

'Yes, Dylan from beyond the grave,' said Bernard, his eyes shining.

'What would you need for it to happen?' Peter asked.

'Dylan Thomas's death mask.'

I winked at Bernard and he smiled.

2

Bernard, Peter and I smuggled the head of Dylan Thomas out of the building a week later.

At the end of the open mic evening, Peter 'forgot' to give the key back to the Dylan Thomas Centre. They knew him so well that no questions were asked.

At five to seven, Bernard parked his car on the paved area in front of the centre. We covered Dylan's bust in bubble wrap, lifted it onto a trolley. In order to get some purchase on the head, I gripped the poet's nose.

The plan was that Bernard could have the sculpture for one night in order to do a 3D scan of Dylan's features. He was to have it back by the time the centre opened next morning. I hardly slept that night for worrying. What if Bernard dropped the head and dented it? Or worse, what if the nose was squashed? What if Bernard were an international art thief? Or if he sold the head to a scrap metal dealer?

I was up far earlier than usual. Sick with anxiety, I left for work without having anything for breakfast. I hung around the front of the Dylan Thomas Centre. Shortly before eight, Bernard dashed into the lobby rolling Dylan Thomas's head in a Sainsbury's trolley. By five past, we'd manoeuvered Dylan back onto his plinth and Bernard had left the premises.

I was glad, after work at the gallery, to have something to do to stop me thinking about Peter and his problems, whatever they were. Bernard had booked a session at the university digital workshop with technician Bruno, where he had computer time to work on his 3D Dylan. Sitting at home watching *Emmerdale* with my parents did not appeal. They kept my bedroom so cold that I had to join them in the lounge if I wanted to feel my extremities. The machines kept the editing suite warm and Bernard didn't seem to mind having me around. His enthusiasm was infectious because the process was pioneering. I don't know why I continued to turn up every night, there was little for me to do besides making endless cups of tea. Bernard and Bruno were so excited that they forgot to drink them, so the cups went cold – but I had a sense that my fate was wrapped up in this project and that, sooner or later, I would have a crucial contribution to make.

We fell into a routine. After work, I'd walk up through town to the university and we'd order in pizza to the editing suite, staying there, glued to the monitors until the early hours of the morning. All I could think of was how much of a gift this would be for poor, dispirited Peter. I followed as best I could so that, when the time came to unveil our triumph, I could give a good basic account of the technology involved.

To begin with, there was very little to see, so I brought my knitting. It seemed to take the computer operator an age to digest the 3D image that Bernard and Bruno had captured of the Dylan Thomas death mask. Bruno told me that they'd made a 3D point cloud of the whole head, polygonised the image and translated it to an STL file for later.

'See, we're making a sort of Dylan clone,' he gushed. I didn't understand at all but made encouraging noises. About ten days in, Bernard and Bruno hit a snag.

Bernard explained: 'See, what we need next is to put flesh on this polygon mesh, so that he looks alive. Virtual skin. Can't use mine because of the beard.'

'Don't look at me,' said Bruno, 'Dylan Thomas wasn't black.'

Bernard narrowed his eyes: 'He had quite a baby face.'

'Hm,' agreed Bruno. 'And we're going to need a pair of lips and eyes to sync in with the reading. A fair approximation.'

'Yeh, they've got to have the right kind of pudginess. A Thomas pout.'

While I was out making tea, I looked at myself in the toilet mirror. I took off my glasses so I could see my eyes properly. They were the right round shape. If I put my hair on top of my head, the ends looked like Dylan's curls.

I addressed myself in the mirror: 'You know, you should get contact lenses. You look great without your specs.'

The truth was that I hadn't altered anything about my appearance for years. Everything I owned was practical. Yes, I hid behind my hair, which I kept long, so that it didn't require trimming every six weeks. I chose specs frames for sturdiness rather than looks, didn't know any other way. If I changed one thing, it might all have to go, and where would I be then?

It would be so good if we could take a mock-up of the head to show Pete. I recalled his sagging shoulders. I wanted to see him smile at me again. I made my decision.

3

The spotlight blazed in my face, dazzling me. I was sat on a stool in the tiny studio surrounded by black.

In order to prepare, I'd spent the whole day listening to arecording of Thomas reading 'And death shall have o dominion' on my old Sony Walkman. I had recorded it so that I had a whole audio cassette filled with nothing but that poem. I tried to match my lips to Thomas's rhythm. In no time at all, I had the poem off by heart. To begin with, I was shocked by the hamminess of Thomas's delivery. His parents had sent him for elocution lessons, I felt sure. I was surprised at how English he sounded, posh even. He had a fine theatrical voice and he played to the gallery:

'Though they go mad they shall be sane,
Though they sink through the sea they shall rise again.'

When I was sure that nobody was in the gallery, I began to recite out loud with Thomas:

'Though lovers be lost love shall not;
And death shall have no dominion.'

Thomas's hypnotic voice, thundering in my ears that death would have no dominion. Never mind that I hated living at home, death would have no… Never mind that Peter, whose wrists I loved and who never wore gloves, and wasn't ever likely to touch me, 'death shall have…' Never mind the solstice dark, the damp Swansea air, 'death shall have no dominion.'

I was a little early at the studio. Bruno had set up the equipment but had disappeared to get a cup of tea. He'd left on a recording of Thomas reading my favourite poem. I sneaked in. There, on the stool, was the contraption which was to fit over the person who was going to 'be' the death mask's features. A friend of Bruno's was due to come in later to model the poet's face, to match the facial movements to the 1950s recording of Thomas's voice. But I couldn't wait. My fingers itched, those restless fingers. Try as I might, I couldn't resist picking the whole thing up and playing with the straps. Quickly, surreptitiously, I slipped it over my head.

Now Dylan's voice coming from the studio speakers sounded as though he and I were in a cathedral together. I knew the recording so well that there was no seam between the booming voice and the movement of my own lips. It wasn't my fault that the red record button was suddenly pressed. I mouthed the words, and Dylan spoke. And that's when it happened.

For a moment, it was as if the world stalled, missed a beat. Under the Mumbles pier, seaweed flipped over inside a wave, the moon bowed to a comet far away and there was an uncanny lull in the Oystermouth traffic. The wind held its breath, then started again, and everything was different. If you believe, as I do, that the watershed dividing the living from the dead is a ridge much less than an atom wide, then the slightest asymmetry draws down the soul to one side or another. A new rhyme sounded between two lives. Something was conjured into play and when the poem released me again, gravity was different. Something looked back at me from behind those words.

The lad who came in to be Dylan's skin was, as far as I was concerned, nothing like him. As Bernard and Bruno saw him to the door, I whipped out his tape and put the take I'd recorded earlier into the player. I kept quiet when they were surprised that the meshing of visual and audio was far more successful than they'd thought at the time. Bruno declared: 'That's it, we've got it.'

Bernard announced that they now had all the pieces they required to create their virtual Dylan. They were like men inspecting a trap they'd set for a very rare creature which had crept in and was breathing, hiding, elsewhere in the room.

4

The first thing I noticed was the hunger.

I sneaked into the kitchen, trying not to make a noise. Mam hated being woken once she'd gone to bed.

I made straight for the cupboard where she kept the breakfast cereals. I plunged my hand into the beige container marked Porridge and stuffed a fistful of the flakes down my gullet. I swallowed with difficulty and found myself scooping another handful to my lips. I pulled out some packets, searching for raisins. Ribena. With hot water. I hadn't had that since I was very young, at home with a cold. Then I had a better idea. I fancied bread and milk – mentioned by Dylan Thomas as the supreme hangover cure.

I wasn't quite sure how to make it. Boil milk in a saucepan and just pour it over stale bread. I needed sugar. And a knob of butter. I could hardly wait for the milk to warm but ripped the crust of a Hovis loaf into a bowl. Then, just as the milk was about to boil over, I whipped if off the hob and poured it with a flourish. Before going to bed, I carefully washed, dried and put the dishes away.

The following morning, I was ravenous again. I usually cowered at the breakfast table, mumbling over a cup of black coffee and trying to avoid Mam's questions about the day to come. My modest bowl of Weetabix was usually more than enough for me, but this time, I heard myself announcing with an enthusiasm which surprised me: 'Now then! Big day today. Dale Plascher and Juliet Lamorgue are reading for our poetry circle tonight. How about a cooked breakfast?'

Mam had let her standards slip recently, I thought. She wasn't enthused by my wanting a full English, so I had to make do with six bowls of Sugar Puffs.

I felt most energetic and decided to walk into the art gallery for work instead of catching the bus. This made me late but for once I didn't care. It was as if the distance between me and the world had slightly altered. I was a match for the raw wind which had brought out early snowdrops. My stride lengthened with joy, and I felt myself to be a fitting frame through which to watch the Uplands gardens. Buds on the trees had swollen noticeably since yesterday, and though there was damp in the air, the lichen on the north sides of winter-sodden trees was drying out, ready for sunshine. I felt a stirring that I can only call spring fever and a conviction that something hugely exciting was about to happen. Was I feeling the beginning of my affair with Peter, at last? I decided that I would declare my passion to him that night.

I was starving again and took myself to the market, bought a carton of cockles and larva bread and ate them on the street with a spoon. That evening I arrived early at the open mic venue, hoping to ambush Peter as we set out the chairs. He wore a new shirt, which I presumed was in honour of the two poets reading that night. He'd cut himself shaving and I thought I smelt a whiff of cologne. With a heart-breakingly eloquent gesture, Peter swept off his glasses and rubbed his beautiful eyes. I could see his long, dark lashes and my heart lurched. I tried to talk to him then, but he seemed nervous. Then bloody Dale Plascher arrived early from London. Peter sent Dale to the restaurant where we were due to eat before the reading while he waited for Juliet, who was coming by car.

The Taj Mahal was cold when we arrived. It was too early in the evening for them to switch on their central heating, so the long red room was warmed by a two-element electric heater over the waiter's station. Dale Plascher studied the menu carefully, but I didn't need to. I knew what I wanted – a lot of everything. When the waiter asked us if we wanted any starters Dale answered confidently, 'Yes. A pint and some poppadoms.'

I like a man who knows how to sink bitter, so I relaxed. I knew it was going to be a good night.

Now I don't normally drink, but somehow, that evening, the beer slid down my throat. Dale Plascher was one of those ugly men who begins to look all right after the third pint. This was partly because he pursued every female fate threw in his path, without discrimination, on the grounds that, by the law of averages, someone, somewhere, was bound to take pity on him. I normally find this dispiriting but tonight it was highly entertaining. I felt attractive, and enjoyed my own curves and Dale's eyes on them. Because I'm not used to drinking a lot, the bubbles went to my head and I began to laugh with what I thought was a fetching tinkle.

I felt a draft as the door opened and Peter entered the restaurant with two women in tow. Juliet, the poet, was a willowy woman about half my size. I didn't catch what the other girl, Susan, did, but I hated her instantly. She slid into the booth next to Peter. She was blonde and lovely. I could feel the cold air on their clothes and, for a moment, it sobered me.

'Come on! You've got some catching up to do!' cried Dale.

I decided to take a break. On my way to the Ladies, I stumbled. The walls bowed towards me and I had to concentrate on walking straight.

When I got back, Juliet was addressing herself to what appeared to be a plate of salad. She had the knack of making everyone on the table watch her hands toying with a string of lettuce in an elegant, delicate fashion. I dipped my finger into the lime pickle and licked.

'I've been reading the Imagists,' she lisped. 'I'm horrified by how underrated H.D. is. That crystalline talent, her pursuit of the pre-feminist orgasm of the mind and soul. She's much better than Pound.'

I turned to Peter, hoping to catch amusement in his eye. Disappointingly, he was nodding earnestly, so I ordered another round of drinks. Then I had a sudden inspiration. I told Dale about the Poet's Game. He leant over to Juliet and whispered in her ear, 'Who would you rather sleep with? Ezra Pound or TS Eliot?'

Juliet cocked her head in what I thought was going to be the start of a withering look but which changed, midstream, into amused consideration.

'You don't have to play this stupid game,' said Peter.

Juliet ignored him, her mouth in a moue. 'That's easy. Got to be Eliot. Pound would give you notes on your performance! You'd get the blue pencil through the long boring bits!'

'Right, you've got to give us another choice,' said Dale, lighting a cigarette, despite Juliet's black looks. Juliet thought for a second.

'I've got one. Shakespeare or Milton?'

Juliet waved Dale's smoke away but looked pensive.

Dale prevaricated: 'Wait, this is a trick one. I'm going to go for Milton.'

'Your reasons?' said Juliet.

'For starters, Shakespeare swung both ways, so you'd never be sure....'

'Fair point. I bet Milton was dirty – all that repression. What with him being blind, sex would be different. You wouldn't have to think how you looked!'

Peter looked at his watch and tried to attract the waiter's attention. I thought for a moment, then had an idea of genius. I whispered it to Dale: 'Emily Dickinson ... Or Emily Brontë?'

Juliet took some time to consider. 'The Brontës would smell rather ... of the manse. All that tiny writing ... I'll go for Emily Dickinson. I think she'd be really wild in bed, once you got her out of that white dress.'

She turned to Peter. 'Have we got time for another drink?'

By the time we got to the Centre, things were very merry. As we entered the hall, Dale was recounting a scandalous story about a public figure who'd been caught in a compromising position with a chicken and Juliet had succumbed to a fit of the giggles which didn't subside even after Peter gave a solemn introduction to their work and distinguished careers.

The reading passed in a blur for me because I'd eaten and drunk so much. I sat at the back so that I could slip out to the loo, as the beer had played havoc with my bladder. I was too drunk to listen to the poems – I stared instead at Peter sitting in the front row with Susan beside him. I watched her blonde head bob towards his, as they exchanged private comments. I stared in disbelief as he smiled and flirted. After the reading was over, he made sure she had a drink. They sat close together in the pub. At closing time I decided that I would follow Dale and Juliet to find a club. Peter said that he would take Susan home and I knew they'd be holding hands as they walked down to the station and my blood ran dark with sadness so I drank some more and danced down low and dirty with Juliet. Thereafter things appeared to me in stills: me sitting in Juliet's tiny lap while we declared our undying love for each other; a clumsy clinch with Dale and – oh God – me stripping on the dance floor.

5

It's impossible to be sick quietly. If your parents' bedroom is next door to the bathroom and the flush has always been temperamental, then there's no chance of keeping drinking a secret.

When I was eventually able to lie down in bed, the room whirled in two different directions. I focused hard on the corner of the wardrobe, trying to hold it steady. I slept. I heard my parents going about their Saturday routine: shopping for groceries in the market, washing done and hung out by noon. I knew that, once I attained consciousness, nothing but pain awaited me, so I concentrated on staying under its surface, like a pike in a pond.

I was still wearing my clothes from the night before, aside from my trousers, which I'd taken off and left in the bathroom. My breath was rank enough to stun a monkey. The afternoon drew to a close, the sound of children playing on the street was dying away as teatime and sports results drew them into warm kitchens.

It was then that I noticed that something else was with me in my fetid subconscious pond. All of a sudden I felt a hand slide under my blouse. I stiffened. The hand paused. Then after an interval, like a cat making its way to the warmest place it can find on a body, it moved again round the back, towards my bra strap.

Clearly, the alcohol I'd consumed at the nightclub had accomplished some serious nerve damage. I turned, making much of rolling right on my back, to blot out any false sensation on the surface of my skin. I settled and waited and so, fell asleep again.

My dreams became sensual. I was being admired and wanted by a persistent nudge that pushed into armpit, nipple and mouth, like the octopus tentacles in erotic prints of Japanese female pearl divers. I was dressed in a loincloth and nothing else, and currents tugged at the material, making it unravel sensually around me. A giant sea slug sucked and slid its way up my thighs, parting and separating, pushing in…

'Get off me, you pervert!' I shouted and started awake, horrified to discover that the bedclothes had been flung off me and my clothes were actually in disarray. Granted, my socks were still on my feet but my extra large knickers were pulled down around my hips. I snatched the sheet and covered myself.

I heard Mam shout after me as I slammed the back door. It was dusk and the street lights came on again. I'd missed a whole day in which people had kept hair salon appointments, bought and sold bric-à-brac in car boot sales, attended sports fixtures, walked dogs, taken young children to swimming pools then parties. I'd done none of these things but something momentous had happened.

Cwmdonkin Park was already closed by the time I reached the gate. I walked round the railings till I found a way that I hadn't used since childhood. I needed to feel cool air on my throbbing head. I made my way to the pond and the sight of regimented municipal roses began to soothe my alcoholic remorse. What pained me wasn't my drunken exploits in the pub and the club after the reading. No, I'd never see Dale or Juliet again. What hurt was the sight of Peter with that girl. Why couldn't he see me?

I am a large woman or 'big-boned' as Mam likes to call it. In my stockinged feet – and those and my hands are large – I'm taller than most men. I've an ample bosom which arouses fascination in young children and drunks. Often I find my embonpoint a convenient shelf on which to rest my hand in stray moments of contemplation. In Welsh, I'd be called a 'noble woman', meaning handsome in a masculine way. My nose is long and straight and I have what I believe to be sensual earlobes, though they're most often hidden behind my long hair. This is no use to me. What I want is to be small and pretty, dainty even. Instead, I was given strength and can carry a double-bed frame on my own down a flight of stairs. I have girth and heft, like a fine piece of industrial engineering. In school I learned to sink into one hip to stand next to the tiny feminine girls who were popular with boys. I had thought more of Pete but he, like all the others, was drawn to a child-bride with big blue eyes, a blonde.

Bereft, I slunk under the willows that swept their hair into the reservoir. I leant against one tree trunk and sank down until I was sitting on my heels. This made my knees pudge out. I was just too solid, too full of flesh to make any man want me.

'Hello, treacle!' said a familiar voice.

I looked round. There was nobody, though I felt sure that I saw a figure reflected in the corner of my glasses. I knew I should have been on my guard against flashers, but the humiliations of the previous night were still pressing on me and I couldn't care less if I was about to be robbed or beaten up.

'If you're wanting to ravish me, all I can say is Good Luck.' I slid down even further and let my buttocks rest on a willow root.

Nobody appeared, so I carried on with my despairing thoughts. Perhaps if I went on a diet? No, my condition required a structural revamp. Was there an operation to shorten your bones? Make you petite?

'Some men have got no taste,' the voice came again, much closer this time. No, surely not. The voice was gravelly, slightly louche, with an old-fashioned pronunciation: 'Why go for quail when you can have suckling pig?'

'Who are you calling a suckling pig?' By now, the hair on my nape was rising but instead of making me frightened, it only added to my rage. 'How dare you? What gives you the right to have an opinion? You've had far too much of my time already for me to have to put up with you any more.'

'But my darling girl, I meant it as a compliment!'

'I know I'm feeling down right now, but I'm not so desperate for male attention that I need flattery from a...'

'Go on, say it.'

'Well, I don't know.'

'You do. Just say it.'

'From a clapped-out poet who's most famous for being drunk and a bum.'

'I know you're hung over, but there's no need to take it out on me.'

'And what about me? I didn't ask to see you. I'm not even a fan of your work. All that death and music.'

'Oh, you can be harsh.'

'And what was that this morning in bed? What are you, a succubus? Groping a woman in her sleep? What next?'

'I think you'll find that I'd be an incubus. A succubus is a female demon. I like the thought of you in a clinch with a lady devil. Didn't you find this morning's dream erotic? Not even a little bit? What I had in mind was a print by Hokusai. Come on, Jennifer, be honest.'

'No! Not even a little. I feel sorry for Caitlin. No wonder she hated you.'

At this, I felt the shade stop and withdraw a little. But now I was well and truly riled.

'She couldn't understand why so many women wanted to sleep with you. She was the handsome one, not you. And she did the difficult job of living on and looking after the family. You were a coward.'

I waited for the orotund reply, ready to find some smart answer to whatever the voice said. Leaves fluttered in the breeze, but all I could see were natural shadows.

I felt suddenly ashamed of my outburst. After all, whatever this voice was – ghost or delusion – it had feelings and could be hurt.

A Gower wind ruffled the surface of the water, setting the roses to gossip in the park. Angry now with myself, I threw a stone into the reservoir.

I shouted, 'Be like that, then. See if I care.'

Nothing.

'I'm sorry!' I called.

My voice echoed over the pavilion and empty tennis courts. Nobody there.

6

That night, in my bedroom, the knocking started. I was stretched out on the bed reading and my parents were out at the Bowling Club. First there was a scuttling sound like mice behind a skirting board. No mouse ever dared enter my mother's house, so I knew who it was and smiled with relief, though I didn't show anything. While I'd been away from home, my mother had kept my childhood bedroom exactly the same, dusting the small ornaments I bought for pennies in jumble sales and church fairs. My collection of glass animals – a fawn, a daschund and a pig – rattled. Next came a blow that made the fringed bedside reading lamp shake.

'I'm too old for poltergeist,' I said. 'You can do better than that.'

Next a pile of my childhood Enid Blytons, squashed between two owl bookends, flew across the room.

'Not to your taste, I know. Why can't we both be adult about this?'

I felt a breath like a feather on my neck.

'And you can knock off the sexual stuff. I don't know how you were allowed to behave in the forties, but groping strangers won't do in the nineties. It's called sexual harassment and it's so passé. You're showing your age.'

'Why don't you make yourself comfortable?' I asked. 'Take a seat.'

I gestured to the old nursing chair to the left of my bed, but didn't lift my eyes from my book. The room went quiet. His voice, when it came, was surprisingly warm: 'I must say, it's a relief not having to perform. It gets so wearing.'

I looked up and there, with a foot propped on his knee and his arms stretched up in a self-conscious pose, sat Dylan Thomas. He wore a bow tie. I held my breath, afraid of scaring the ghost away.

'The thing is, once you get a certain reputation for being bohemian, people expect you to be up to no good.'

'If what I've read about you is true, it would have been better if you'd spent more time writing rather than performing the part of the poet.'

'It was a form of public service. '

'Didn't sound like much fun to me, drinking yourself to death abroad.'

'But people enjoy seeing somebody else live out their fantasies. It saves them from having to be self-destructive themselves. They should pay people like me to do it and then they could pretend they're sorry when you're dead.'

'You make it sound like a sacrifice. You had lots of fun.'

'No, I didn't. I would much prefer to have lived like a librarian. Bread and hot milk at nine. Lights out at ten. Flannelette sheets. But where was the money in that?'

'Are you telling me that hellraiser Dylan was all an act?'

'Of course! Who wouldn't prefer to be in their pyjamas, tucked in bed with a good book than out in a strange city, playing the poet in front of strangers? One of my great regrets is that I never got to finish the matchstick model of the *HMS Victory* on which I was engaged when fate so cruelly intervened...'

This was a totally new Dylan to me.

'... Not to mention the model of St Paul's Cathedral. I'd just found a way of doing the dome. I was about to double-dig the allotment too. Caitlin never got to grips with the vegetables. Did you know that I was a champion folk dancer? I had to do that under a pseudonym – Derek Thomas – but I was really rather good.'

'Look, my parents are going to be back from Bowls soon, why are you here?'

Dylan Thomas's girth made the nursing chair look slight. His body language had changed when he discussed his hobbies and he was now sitting up straight, with his knees together. 'I presume that a dead poet doesn't appear to the living for no reason.'

He straightened his jacket. 'Your surmise is correct. There are things that need to be learned.'

'What do you want from me Mister Thomas?' I asked, thinking that a more formal approach might suit the occasion.

'For one thing, death does have quite a lot of dominion, I have found.' Thomas studied his nails. 'Oh yes indeedy.'

'Doesn't have the same ring, does it? So have you come back to alter your work?'

'No, force majeur. No choice. Command performance. Hence the bow tie.'

'If you're worried, your reputation is still good. You seem to get more famous by the year, not less.'

'The thing about death is that it's very hard to accept, even when you're dead. Maybe especially then.'

'Mind you, I think that people know more about your rackety life than read your poems.'

For the first time, the ghost appeared perturbed. 'Don't they study me in schools and universities?'

'They do. But you're known as one of the Three Thomases.'

'There are others?'

'Yes, Edward Thomas, and then RS. He lived into his eighties. He wrote a lot about God.'

'Was he known for being drunk on language like me?'

'No. A vicar. Clean-living. Liked ornithology.'

'Is he better known than me?'

'Nominated for the Nobel.'

'Bugger.'

'You were telling me why I've been graced with your presence.'

Now he was distracted. 'Poems any good?'

'Superb.'

'I could do birds.'

'Yes, but you didn't. You were too busy making a name for yourself in America.'

'Just because I'm dead doesn't mean that I've stopped writing poems. In fact, I've been working really hard.'

'You're thought of as a poet addicted to sound – more music than sense.'

'But my new work addresses that. You'd be surprised. I've pared it all down. My haiku are great. I bet they'd be well received.'

'Put them away! What *is* it with poets, always pulling out their pieces?'

'But sweetheart, I'm not just any poet, I'm *the* poet.'

'Face it, your reputation is never going to go any higher.'

'But if you found a batch of manuscripts lost until now…'

'That's cheating. If you were allowed to write from beyond the grave, what would the other poets think? They'd all want to do it.'

'Oh, go *on*. I've got just the job – a history of the steam engine in hexameters.'

'Out of the question. You're dead. Accept it.'

'I could make it worth your while.'

'All I want is for you to disappear. I've got enough problems without being sexually molested by a spook.'

'Look, I'll do anything. Don't you understand? All a poet ever really cares about is his reputation.'

'Why should I help you?'

In his impatience, Dylan Thomas's knees began to jig up and down and he rattled some coins in his trouser pocket. A sly look came over his face.

'I could help you with Peter.'

'I don't need any help,' I said wanly but I knew straight away that I was on shaky ground. I heard myself ask, 'What could you do?'

'I could get him to sit up and pay some attention to you.'

I didn't want to appear to be too eager, so I tried a diversionary tactic: 'I'm sure that isn't why you came here. Get back to that reason.'

Thomas leant forward in his chair. He mopped beads of sweat from his upper lip and forehead.

'Forget that. This is far more pressing. I could make you the most important person in Peter's life. Imagine yourself in his arms. By the time I'm finished, he'll be licking cream out of your belly button.'

'Don't. You're disgusting. Really?'

'By the muse of the Cymric and Britannic…'

'Oh, don't start. By the way, I thought you'd talk like that all the time.'

'Like what?'

'You know. All poetic and rhetorical.'

'I'm out of practice. You think the dead don't change? I like to keep up with how people speak. I've got a good ear. You'll have to help me clean up my name.'

'Can we get back to my love life?'

I took a deep breath.

'All right. I'll help you and in return, you get me Peter and then you go back to your grave and leave us alone.'

The ghost licked his finger: 'Cross my heart and hope to live.' Then he disappeared.

From downstairs I heard the front door.

'Yoo hoo! We're home!'

Then my father mumbled something under his breath about my mother forgetting. I ignored them and turned on my side to dream about Peter and how he would smell when he kissed me for the first time.

7

'What we need,' said Dylan Thomas, 'is a manuscript factory.'

We were whispering in my bedroom. I lived in fear of my mother hearing our night-time talks, so I tried to tell him to keep his voice down but you try hushing a person who has filled halls in America with what he thinks is his lovely Celtic voice. I dreaded to think what Mam would say to find a man in my room. True, he was fully booted and spurred and, technically, dead but I didn't think that the state of his dress would figure in her reaction. However many times I reminded him, Dylan Thomas would get excited about something and start booming again and that's not to mention the chain-smoking in a Puritan house. It was an uphill struggle. Then I remembered the shack.   ¹

During the Second World War, Swansea was heavily bombed by the Germans, with huge areas of the city destroyed by fire. Residents began to look for ways to escape the heaviest of the raids. Some made agreements with farmers on the nearby Gower Peninsula to allow them to build chalets in fields near the sea. My grandparents built one in Owen's field at Caswell. We used to go down there for summer weekends, but, in recent years, my parents seemed to have forgotten about it. I knew where my mother kept the key. Dylan Thomas and I could use it, a clubhouse – every child's dream. During our nightly sessions in my tiny bedroom,

35

Dylan Thomas had begun to sing, so I had to do something and fast.

We agreed to meet at the chalet after work. The evenings were beginning to lighten, so it wasn't entirely dark when I turned into Summerland Lane and on to the field. My parents' shack was made out of tin sheeting and they'd called it 'Fern Hill'. It could have been worse. 'Balmoral', another of these rickety, higgledy-piggledy huts, was further down the lane. The grass was waist high as I pushed my way to the door. I congratulated myself on remembering to bring some WD40 to ease the padlock. After some jigging about I managed to get the key to turn.

If anything, it was colder inside than out in the light. I felt cobwebs on my face. Luckily, I knew the tiny cabin like the back of my hand because I'd spent many weeks there during student summers, just to get away from home. Soon I had three gas mantles lit, had found the gas heater and put the kettle on. As soon as I did that, Dylan Thomas appeared.

'I'm three sugars,' he said. 'Any biscuits?'

'You can't even eat and you've still got a sweet tooth.'

'Force of habit.'

He lit up and pulled the smoke down deep into his lungs. 'At last, a smoking room!'

'Ashtray!' I scolded as I saw him flick his cigarette ash onto the floor. Then I remembered it wasn't real ash. I bet he did that even when he was alive.

Dylan began by enquiring after my day at work, as if I were a spouse of twenty years or a regular at his local pub. I reminded him sharply that we had business to do.

'This isn't a social occasion, cock. As soon as we've both completed our part of the deal, I won't have to see your podgy face. So I'm not planning on getting to know you well. You said you had an idea. Get on with it.'

With his good cheer entirely undented, Dylan Thomas outlined his plan. Sweeping his arms wide open, and gesticulating to a crowd that wasn't there he roared: 'Chatterton! The marvellous boy! That's the answer to all our problems.'

Dylan beamed. I looked at him blankly.

'Oh, don't tell me. What do they teach in schools these days? Thomas Chatterton, the Bristol enfant terrible? The Rowley poems?'

The names meant nothing to me. Thomas settled himself in the green plaid sofa and prepared to lecture: 'Thomas Chatterton was a young prodigy at the time of the English Romantics. He wanted to make a name for himself in London, and so he claimed to have found some medieval poems written by a monk called Rowley. Only problem was, he forged them.'

Something stirred in my memory. 'Isn't there a famous painting…?'

Dylan Thomas flung himself full-length on the sofa into a pose of ecstatic abandon. 'That's right. Chatterton in an Adam Ant shirt, stretched out, dead, in a garret.'

'Your point is?'

'Chatterton's forgeries were crude. He wrote on pieces of paper, which he rubbed on dirty windowpanes in order to make them appear old. We can do better than that.' I looked dubious. Dylan Thomas righted himself and proceeded to settle into the couch. 'What could go wrong? It's not as if you'd have to make up the poems. You've got the real Dylan Thomas here and I've got stacks! The work's all done, it's just a question of editing.'

'What about handwriting? I don't suppose a ghost can write.'

'No, but we can do that W.B. Yeats thing of automatic

writing. You hold the pen, but the spirit dictates the words. I can guide your hand. That way no calligraphy expert on earth can say that it isn't my work.'

I didn't like the sound of that. 'Will it hurt?'

'I promise to behave, you can have no worries on that score, dear girl. The pleasure will be all mine.'

I thought of another snag. 'What about materials? They can tell a forgery's not genuine by ink and paper analysis.'

'No sweat,' Dylan countered, picking his teeth, though he hadn't actually eaten anything. 'You may not have noticed it, but you're currently residing in a nineteen fifties museum: your parents' house.'

'That's a bit harsh. I'd say more late sixties myself.'

'Does your father or does he not still use the fountain pen he used during the war?'

'He does.'

I began to smile.

'And did the traffic department only recently move and throw out their stationery, which they'd had since the war? And did your father not salvage the bloody lot?'

'Bingo!'

'I rest my case. Now, Jennie darling, all you have to do is obtain some paper, pen and ink, meet me here tomorrow and we'll get to work.'

8

These days when we met, Peter barely spoke, though I did my best to cheer him up with chitchat about this and that. If I hadn't been so in love with him, I'd have thought his silence rude. As it was, I put all that brooding down to his artistic nature. Finally, I became so mystified by what had made Peter sullen that, one Saturday lunchtime, I decided to follow him.

He went to the lounge of the Packet. I peeked through the mullioned glass of the Lounge and my heart sank when I saw him bend over to kiss a girl with blonde hair. Susan. It must be serious. He went to the bar, bought drinks and ordered food. The two were so deep in conversation that I was able to slip into the booth next to them. I could hear their voices through the lunchtime buzz.

'I can't get over it.'

'It's bound to take time,' Susan said squeezing his hand. Stupid girl. What he needs is action, not talk, I thought.

'You mustn't blame yourself.'

'But I do. The whole thing was my stupid idea. If it hadn't been for me, she...'

Just as what he said was getting interesting soppy Susan cut across him. 'Hush, hush, you mustn't think like that. You were doing what you thought was best.'

'We just can't carry on without some money. I'm racking my brains for what we can do, but I can't think of anything that will help.'

This was a shock to me. You can't charge people for an open mic. I hadn't realised that Peter wanted to develop the poetry group into a proper society and publish their poems.

At that point I nearly jumped up and shouted: 'Don't worry! I've got exactly what you need!' But that would have given away the fact that I'd followed him to the pub, so I reined myself in and slipped out before the lovers spotted me. Here was a chance for me to raise money for Peter and get rid of Susan in one fell swoop. For the first time in a few days, I felt glad that I was being haunted by a dead poet.

The sentiment didn't last. That night, at the shack, Dylan Thomas was more than usually chatty, regaling me with jokes while I was trying to tell him how desperate was my true love's thwarted ambition. He pestered me like a child.

'Come on, Jennie! Bet you haven't heard this one. Right. What do you call a man who's been buried for six centuries?' he asked.

I began to say that we needed to get down to work, but there was no way out.

'I don't know. What *do* you call a man who's been buried for six centuries?'

Dylan Thomas leaned back and cackled. 'Pete! D'you get it? Peat!'

That did it. 'Look! I'm fed up of being polite. You've had your love life and you made a right mess of it. Mine hasn't even begun and I intend to get my man.'

Dylan Thomas took a huge cigar from his pocket and made much of lighting it. I flung the writing materials that I'd filched from home onto the table.

'I've done my part, now it's up to you. I hope you've been polishing some nice new poems. After all, you've got nothing to do all day except be dead. I've got to go to work.'

'Actually,' said Dylan Thomas, drawing on his cigar and blowing smoke rings, 'being dead is quite hectic.'

'That's ridiculous. What on earth is there for you to do?'

'Well, it takes a long time to recover from dying, you know. Especially if it was unforeseen. I mean, I didn't have a clue what had happened. One minute I was in New York, and the next I was dead. Hell of a shock.'

'And are they treating you well?' I asked sarcastically. Then, ashamed of myself, I asked, 'What's it like?'

He answered, 'You should know. I thought I'd be left alone to rest, as they say, in peace, but there's lots of meeting and greeting and people talking all the time. It's terribly confusing. No wonder I'm having trouble—'

'Doing what?'

'Oh, nothing. Sleeping. Can't get a wink. They've put all us poets together. Frankly, I thought it would be great to meet Shakespeare but he wrote so much when he was young that he wants nothing to do with literature. He's obsessed with hare coursing. Milton, though, was a big surprise. Blind as a bat but full of fun. The peat joke is his.'

'That doesn't sound right. I thought everyone would be very solemn.'

'They're very keen on self-development. You have to evolve,' he made a large gesture, 'or you're left for dead. And that you don't want.'

'And is haunting me part of how you,' I copied his gesture, 'evolve?'

'Yes, though this project has taken an unofficial turn which I'm keeping from Him.'

'Does Him mean God?'

'No, stupid. My Project Manager. A bit like the way I'm managing you.'

GWYNETH LEWIS

'You're not managing me. I'm letting you into my life, though God knows why.'

'And then there's Physical Education.'

'You do exercises?'

'Not exactly. I find the yoga's very good. You see, our bodies are not the same as those of the living. There's a period when you look and move pretty much the same as when you died. But then you start changing.'

'Will you start rotting and appear to me one night with your eye hanging out of its socket?'

'This isn't my corpse you're seeing, it's my spirit. Oh, it's difficult to describe. You'll see.'

'Look, can we get down to work? I haven't got all night. My parents will be double-locking the front door soon and there'll be trouble if I have to wake them up to get into the house.'

Dylan Thomas hauled himself up from the sofa. He looked slimmer and I noticed that his shirt was ironed. His manner became business-like.

'Right. I haven't done this dictating thing before but I asked Yeats about it and he said it's a piece of cake. Just empty your mind and let me...'

I protested, 'You're standing far too close.'

'Do you want to do this or not? How many millions of people would love to have me, druid of the broken body, dictating poetry to them? I turn down requests all the time from some very prominent people.'

'I still don't trust you.'

'Just let me in and I'll guide your hand. If you want your Peter, it's the only way...'

I uncapped the fountain pen and took a deep breath.

9

'Is it me?' I asked, doing my very best to be tactful, 'or is this not very good?'

We were at the shack and we were looking over the poems we'd produced the previous night. Dylan Thomas became defensive.

'What would you know? It looks strange to you because it's part of my late style and, therefore, groundbreaking. Trust me, that's what the critics will say.'

From elsewhere on Owen's Field Eminem sounded out through the dark Gower night. This was turning out to be an awkward conversation. I would rather have dropped it, but I wasn't willing to risk my future with Peter for fear of offending Dylan Thomas. I trod carefully.

'I hear what you're saying but listen to this.'

I lifted one of the manuscript pages so that I could read it by gaslight. "I scry the dulse, whose pulse plies me/ With ozone-argon agonies." Can that be right?'

'Perfect example of the influence of the Welsh *cynghanedd* on yours truly, I'd say.'

'It sounds good, but what does it mean?'

Dylan Thomas became agitated. This was very delicate, but I soldiered on.

'I don't know, but sounds as though this writer's read too much Dylan Thomas.'

'I *am* Dylan Thomas,' he said, exasperated.

'Yes, but you can have too much of a good thing.'

The party music thudded louder. Dylan Thomas strode to the shack door, wrenched it open and shouted, 'Keep the noise down, you wretches. How do you expect me to compose in such a racket?'

'I mean, Dylan Thomas would sound different, less juicy.'

He gave me a withering look. 'You're telling me, one of the creators of the twentieth-century modernist lyric, that I'm derivative?' That was it, basically, but I didn't want to labour the point. Dylan Thomas pulled a sheet from the bottom of the pile.

'Well, what about this one? This is very new for me,' he said.

'Ah, yes, I was meaning to ask you about that one.' I read out loud:

'To be born in Wales…'

'Doesn't it sound just a tad familiar?'

'What are you suggesting? That I'm…'

The rap grew louder. Dylan Thomas ripped open the door and screamed: 'Don't make me come down there and sort you out!'

It made not the blindest bit of difference. If anything, the music was louder. He flung himself back on the couch. 'Honest, this place was lovely and quiet during the war.'

That surprised me. 'Did you come down here much?'

'Yes, one of my girlfriends… That's it! I've had enough. Hand me that golf club. They've got no right…'

'Look,' I said in my most reasonable voice, 'there's no point shouting. That's Julian's hut down there. Six bikers and a sound system from hell. If they decide to party, there's nothing you can do.'

'Bloody riff-raff, ruining the peace for people who are trying to THINK!' And he paced the tiny cabin, making the china tinkle on its shelf.

I continued in a level voice: 'All I want is to find something that will achieve what we want…'

But Dylan Thomas was worked up now. Two pink spots appeared on his cheeks and he began throwing dishes into the sink, as if he were going to wash up.

'You people who don't write, you assume it's easy. Why do you think I needed a garage in Laugharne, perfect peace and quiet? What do you expect me to do in such a racket?'

I didn't point out that it had been quiet last night, when we did the dictation.

'It's not enough for you that we have to live on a pittance. No, you want us to dive into the deep waters of the soul time after time and bring up pearls. Well, you shouldn't be surprised when some of us drown…'

'Calm down!'

'I won't. This is the limit. Not only do I have to babysit you, you're hypercritical…'

'Oh, please don't cry.'

Too late. Embarrassed, I sidled up to the weeping Dylan Thomas and placed my hand on his back. He was mumbling now. 'I did my best, but you don't understand how hard it is to write poetry. '

'Is it writer's block?' I asked very gently.

He nodded without speaking. I patted his shoulder sympathetically. The music at Julian's cabin was building up to rave proportions. I could hear cars full of revellers arriving, and excited shouts from the bonfire they'd spent that afternoon building.

Gradually, Dylan Thomas's sobs quietened to a low snuffling. I racked my brains.

'Is there anything I can do? What if we both sat down?'

'It's hopeless. The truth is, I was finished as a poet even before I died. Why do you think I was running around

America doing all those readings? I'd do anything – ANYTHING – to avoid having to sit down at a desk in front of a blank sheet of paper.'

I made sympathetic noises, as if I knew exactly what it was like to be a washed-up world-class poet.

'You can't imagine the pressure – having to come up with something better all the time, not repeating yourself, it drove me mad.'

Dylan Thomas turned away from the sink and faced me, miserable, as he continued: 'And being dead, well that only made things worse.'

'How so? I'd have thought it would be nice to meet your fellow poets and compare notes on your craft.'

'No!' he wailed, 'It was ten times harder. It's no accident that the collective noun for a group of poets is a "paranoia". If you've ever seen a gang of poets alive, they're bad enough. But imagine the Greats. More touchy, less tolerant and more competitive than anybody else. That's how they got to the top of the pile.'

He bit the knuckle of his clenched fist in an effort to control his voice. It died to a whisper.

'Wordsworth and his lot are horrible bullies…' As he said this, his huge eyes found mine.

I struggled to know what to say. 'Sounds as if … you've lost your confidence a bit.'

'I've lost my nerve completely. That poem you recognised, it's an RS Thomas. I knew you liked him so I thought … and you're right, the other stuff is rubbish. I put it through Babelfish on the web.'

He sat down heavily on the sofa, his head in his hands.

He was a pathetic sight. I sat next to Dylan and took his curly head in my hands and gently laid it to rest on my breast.

Gradually, his breathing became more regular and his body relaxed.

'How would it be if you and I visited some of the places that used to inspire you to write. Do you think that would help?'

I felt his head nod and something like 'yes' in a little boy's voice.

'How about Gower? Can you name a place of which you were especially fond?'

'I liked Worm's Head.'

'Well, then, why don't you go…' The whimpering started again, so I corrected myself, 'why don't *we* go and see what happens? Two heads are better than one.'

I felt a crick in my neck and made to move. The ghost protested: 'No, don't leave me,' so I snuggled back in, stroking the famous auburn hair. Garage music took hold of the shack and shook it.

10

The following day, I called in sick at the gallery so that Dylan and I could go out looking for inspiration at the tip of the Gower peninsula. We'd agreed to leave first thing, but I waited for him for hours and hours, lying on my bed in the shack. Each time I heard someone coming along the lane, I got up, thinking it was him. Revellers from Julian's party passed in dribs and drabs, still wearing last night's clothes and cowed by daylight. It was mid afternoon when, finally, Dylan Thomas arrived.

'Where have you been?' I asked resentfully.

'Big night,' he said, 'tell you about it later.'

It was the tail end of a bright spring day, and at Rhosili, I strode out across the cliff-top, exhilarated to see the long, thin spit of Worm's Head. It looked like a strange sea creature towing the land out into Carmarthen Bay. The wind was warm and carried the nutty smell of gorse in bloom. I heard a cry from behind me and turned to see Dylan Thomas in the distance.

'Wait for me! It's all right for you, you're alive and fit!'

I still hadn't forgiven him for keeping me waiting, so I laughed and broke into a run, stopping only at the lifeguard's station overlooking the headland. Instead of studying the tide tables I sat down in the late afternoon sun listening to the bees in a clump of sea pinks. I felt as though I'd been in a dark, stuffy box for a long time, and only now was I able to breathe.

Eventually, Dylan Thomas collapsed next to me, gasping. I could see his man boobs heaving under his shirt. I hauled myself up and offered him my hand. 'Come on!' I urged, 'let's make the most of the light.'

We made quick work of the stretch of rocks which led out to headland, picking our way around pools and clumps of mussels. There was a path along the first part of the peninsula, which looked like the first coil of the monster facing the channel. A narrow ridge of rocks linked the worm's body to its head. We stood for a moment, contemplating it.

'I don't know,' said Dylan Thomas, 'all it would take is a twisted ankle and we're done for.' I inched my way out, determined to reach the tip.

'You're a ghost, you haven't got an ankle to sprain.'

I started crawling across the rocks on all fours. I glanced up and saw Dylan Thomas mincing his way across the ridge.

'The secret is not to put your weight down!'

Soon he'd passed me. When I reached the tip of the worm, I joined him where he lay on his stomach looking down at the waves roaring their applause. We didn't speak for the longest time.

When I woke, I was alone. The breeze had turned keen and I was in shadow. I looked out to sea. The water was striped, because banks of cloud had moved in from the west. Dylan Thomas was nowhere to be seen, but I hoped that he'd been taking notes about the cormorants drying themselves on the rocks below or perhaps about the circular breathing of the sea. He was the poet, it was up to him to come up with the artistic goods. I looked at my watch. Time to go.

I found him sitting forlorn on a rock looking at the land. Beyond him, where the tide had come in, had become a sound.

The full horror of our situation sank in. We were stranded. I asked, 'How long will it be before we can cross?'

'Ten hours,' said Dylan, his voice like lead. We were cut off from the mainland until the following morning. 'Why didn't you check the tide tables?'

'You could just have easily have checked.'

'You were in charge of this trip, it was all your idea. I didn't really want to come, you made me.'

This was too much to bear. 'I didn't force you. I was trying to help. Besides, if you hadn't been hours and hours late we'd have had all afternoon…'

Dylan Thomas rounded on me, his tone sulky: 'It's not as if looking after you is my only duty. I've got other things to do, people to see.'

The prospect of spending the night on the headland made me short-tempered: 'I thought it was me looking after you. Don't bother yourself on my behalf…'

The poet hunched against the gathering cold and turned up the collar on his suit. 'That's rich. You're using me. Never mind that I'm suffering Post Traumatic Stress Disorder from dying. Oh no, all you want is a poem. You're push, push, push!'

'A half-decent writer could come up with a lovely little poem about this place. You're not up to the job and you never were.'

'Well, clever clogs, you pretend that you're so into poetry. If you'd done your homework, you'd have realised that I've already written about Worm's Head.'

'I don't believe you.'

'A short story about exactly this, being stranded out here for the night. And I've got news for you: there are rats.'

'Oh, that's great, just what I need. You're a grown man, you have a tongue. And you didn't think to tell me that you've done Worm's Head before we came all this way.'

'Why should I? You were so wrapped up in producing a new manuscript, you haven't been listening to me.'

'That's hardly surprising when you do nothing but moan.'

'Oh, that's rich. All I'm trying to do is help.'

'Help? As far as I can see, all you worry about is your own reputation.'

'I couldn't care less about that. When will you get it into your stupid head that I'm here because you need guidance? The deal is, I get you back and they give me a stab at a second career.'

'I'm not going anywhere, so you can leave me alone.'

'You're completely at sea and you don't even know it.'

'You're a poet. You're unqualified to do anything else but be a bum and a waster.'

Before I met Dylan Thomas I'd have sworn that ghosts don't feel temperature, but my companion was shivering, a tinge of blue appearing around his lips and the mouth. I softened my voice and said, 'Let's move from here, it's getting cold.'

We made our way up the rocks and found a small hollow out of the wind and settled down together. I wasn't willing to let my point go: 'Face it, you're useless. Writing's all you know.'

He mumbled something. I had to ask him to repeat it because I didn't believe what I'd heard. He said it again. 'I want to do an ultra-marathon.'

Above us a gull called before making its way back to its warm nest.

'I told you I never settled with the poets. Wordsworth and Coleridge are always ganging up on me and none of the others take my side – even Ted Hughes joins in and calls me names and him a Johnny-Come-Lately! People like him are all cragginess and spare thoughts. They're lean of line and jaw.

I don't fit in. Look at me: all curls and blubber. I like ornamentation and a good sing-song. Maybe it's because I'm Welsh. But that's not in fashion. No, they all hate me. The only one who was friendly in the least was Gerard Manley Hopkins. He's Christian, he's got to love everyone, so it hardly counts and, quite frankly, he was hard to get close to, what with all those nuns around him. Oh, and Christopher Smart was nice, but he's delusional. They were always picking on me – Robert Southey too – and they sent me to Coventry as a joke. So I ran away to the athletes' place.'

'You mean they're all together as well?'

'It's a different wavelength and I found I could tune myself in. It's like the light spectrum, all the souls are at different frequencies. Master Blacksmiths on one, Chess Grand Masters a fraction onwards, Chefs next – you get the idea. You're meant to stay among your own kind, but I hated mine. Soon as I found the athletes, I felt so much better.'

'But you're the most unsporty person I've ever met.'

'Give me a chance, I need time to train. Thing is, I fell in with a bunch of the Tarahumara, those Mexican Indians who run without shoes. They showed me how to do it.'

'Barefoot? But you're a chain-smoker!'

'Have you seen me smoking today? See, you have to release your inner runner, that part of you that's been bred for millennia to hunt by out-chasing your prey on the plains.'

'Well, I would never have predicted this.'

'No shoes and a faster pace than usual. You run at slightly more than two steps per second. It's entirely natural.'

'But you're totally out of shape. A sprint would kill you.'

'That's why you have to train. And they've said that if I do the work, they'll take me as an honorary member of the tribe. But they recognised me as one of their own. I think it's the rhythm. Just think! I've been ticking over at one hundred and eighty beats per minute all this time and I didn't know it! In poetry, it makes your lines fussy. But running on a plain, I can hit my stride.'

'This is ridiculous. I don't even want to think about this. Why exactly do you have to be part of a group?'

'You can't go through death alone. We're not designed for it. You have to have company. That's why choirs do so well in the afterlife. All those concerts and music. We're social animals. And I want to run.'

'It's all about what you want to do, isn't it, Dylan?' I replied bitterly.

'If I could be stretched as a runner, I'm sure I could write a new poetic line. I have an artistic hunch about this. Those instincts are always right.'

My sunny mood of earlier had entirely evaporated. The prospect of freezing in the dark with a poet who'd just come out as a long-distance runner was doing nothing to improve my spirits. We didn't even have a flask of tea to cheer us up. I told him that he needed to choose between his ambitions for his posthumous reputation as a poet and his desire to join the select company of ultra-marathon runners.

'I don't see why one couldn't combine both careers,' he whined. 'Why don't we forge a hitherto undiscovered collection of Dylan Thomas's sports journalism, including a classic essay about Wales' famous victory over the All Blacks in 1953? You're such a killjoy. You ask the man on the street what gives him pleasure. It's sport, it combines everything important: struggle, death, defeat and victory.

'Poetry's a severe mistress. If you don't dedicate yourself to the art before all else, then the Muse isn't going to treat you right.'

'You should be glad for me that I'm able to see a career for myself beyond death,' he said, changing tack. 'I mean, there's no reason to regard dying as the end of the road. It could be the start of a whole new life.'

'That's taking positive thinking to a ridiculous extreme. When I'm dead, I'm retiring for good.'

'But think of the opportunities! You could discover whole new parts of yourself.'

'What part of dead don't you understand?'

'You're thinking too narrowly, hemming yourself in. That's the beauty of dying, you get liberated from these confining ideas.'

'You're making no sense. What are you? A careers officer for corpses?'

'Now that you mention it…'

'Don't tell me that such a thing exists.'

'There you go again, contempt before investigation. Jennie, you're so quick to dismiss what you think you do and don't like, you're missing the treasures under your nose.'

'I know my mind. And being stuck here with you is the last thing I need.'

'Jennie, I'm on your side.'

'You're no use to me unless you help me get Peter.'

'Oh, honey, wake up. You have no comprehension of your situation, do you?'

At that, I snapped. 'Don't call me stupid. You could do what I want while standing on your head. You were the greatest love poet of the twentieth century. You must have *some* understanding of how the human heart works. For once, use that insight, show some emotional intelligence. Is that too much to ask?'

He didn't answer. Growing up in my parents' house, I'm used to all kinds of manipulative behaviour and emotional blackmail. I can take verbal abuse, I don't care if you call me a failure or a grave disappointment, in fact such language makes me feel on track, that I must be rebelling enough to be a person in my own right. However, there's one thing I can't stand and that's being ignored. I hate the way it wipes you out as a person, excludes you completely from someone else's world. I'll do or say anything to get a reaction, to re-engage a person, to connect. And that's why, that evening, I went too far.

'You may not know this but since the nineteen nineties it's well established that Dylan Thomas only wrote so well because he was impotent.'

We both stopped breathing and I knew that I'd scored a bull's eye. I didn't have the sense to keep quiet, but drove home my advantage.

'There was that letter from one of your American lovers, a girl you met on tour, saying that you were terrible in bed.'

The poet crumpled. He wasn't to know that I'd made up the story. By the time the water had drained from the causeway, allowing us to cross back to the mainland in a mother-of-pearl dawn, we still hadn't talked. At the shack, Dylan Thomas made himself – but not me – a cup of tea, ate the last of the cornflakes then fell asleep diagonally across the cabin's double bed.

When I got back into the house, I found my mother had waited up. She was crying. She'd put on the artificial firelight – but not the electric bar – to comfort herself in the early spring chill. The flicker of the foil fan made her face look strangely soft and young. She cried like a child, as if I weren't there. Outside, in the suburban gardens, the morning light hardened. On the whole, I preferred it when she shouted.

11

Never underestimate the capacity of a poet to sulk.

My sleep was shot through with an emotion I didn't recognise at first. After a couple of hours' restlessness, I got up to shower. It was shame. I'd hit my friend below the belt. By the next day, I was desperate to make up with Dylan but he didn't come. I decided that I'd seen the last of him, and that, if I was going to pursue Peter, from now on I'd have to rely on my own resources.

I happened to be passing the Centre that lunchtime, and noticed a poster advertising a meeting of the poetry circle that evening. Odd, that was news to me. When had he set that up? Why hadn't he told me about it? My mind raced. Had I offended him in some way, was he dropping me as an assistant?

I was so mortified that I decided to go to the event in disguise. Confronting Peter was out of the question. I'd have to pick up what I could on the night. I had a blonde wig which I'd bought once to go to an Abba party in London. I'd kept the wig, knowing it would come in handy one day. I took off my glasses and, in the mirror, I looked spookily different. Downstairs, I could hear my parents bustling around, on their way out somewhere. I called to them that I wasn't feeling well and would have a night in and was very relieved when they let me be.

I was late arriving because I'd decided to wear the silver boots that went with the Abba wig. I thought they went well with my circular tweed skirt – an ironic juxtaposition which pleased me. By the time I'd reached the corner of our cul de sac, I was in agony, but there was no time to go back and change. I hobbled down to the marina, hoping I didn't look too much like a transvestite.

The Centre was packed, so I pushed my way to the back, where there was standing room only. Peter was at the microphone, wearing an unfamiliar tie with his denim shirt. At his feet, in the VIP row, I could see Susan. It was a good thing, I decided, that I'd come. Maybe there was something I could do to keep them apart. I tuned in to what Peter was saying. Something about 'this tribute being the most fitting way to say what we want in the face of tragedy.' It must be a benefit for children in the Third World, another famine or civil war. Peter was always going on about such injustices. He was such a caring person. I felt an upsurge of love for him and the nobility of his nature.

My eye caught a sudden movement down the side of the room. It was Dylan Thomas, making his way past the rows of people, towards the reserved seats. I strained to see what he was up to, but my view was blocked. The tall man in front of me shifted on his feet and I nearly choked when I saw that the poet had slipped into a seat next to Susan. Luckily, she hadn't noticed yet as she'd leant over to speak to the elderly couple sitting next to her. There was still time to get rid of him.

I was wrong. Peter cleared his throat and brought out a folded piece of paper from the back pocket of his jeans. He was nervous and looked at Susan for reassurance. As I inched my way down the room, I only caught snatches of what Peter was saying. He was reading a poem:

Words fail but what a fall was here
Where gravity was infinitely grave…

A bit morbid for him, I thought. Then, to my horror, Dylan stood up and stepped onto the platform. I gasped. He was wearing a shell suit. Ever the professional, Peter carried on as if nothing had happened. Dylan Thomas stood at his side and began to do stretches, as if he were warming up for some physical exertion to come. I looked at the audience. They were still concentrating on Peter's words. He was going on about death:

Indifferent to those we hold dear
Possessive of everything she gave.

I pushed my way further forward and was incensed to see Dylan Thomas begin on a yoga routine. Now on all fours, he flexed his spine a few times, looking as though he were making love to a bichon frisée. Then, he grunted loudly as his arse came up into Downward-Looking Dog. His whole body quivered with the effort. From the front of the audience I hissed at him to get off the stage. Then, ignoring me completely, Dylan Thomas lowered himself into Cobra and, looked up at the ceiling.

Peter carried on reading, entirely unperturbed. Poetry events anywhere usually attract at least one, if not more, mental health patients. If they're taking their medication, keep their comments to a reasonable level and don't smell too much, these individuals are welcomed with open arms but, in Swansea, we do have a number to call if dialogues with the devil are in danger of drowning out the featured poet. I slipped out of the room and phoned the emergency mental health team.

The room was deathly quiet when I came back in. Dylan had disappeared. I glanced behind me at the crowd but what I saw made me choke. The elderly couple sitting next to Susan was my parents. But, more than that, Dylan Thomas had sat himself down in Mam's lap and was swinging one leg back and forth like a child. My mother seemed entirely at ease and was concentrating on Peter's words.

I looked around, desperate. I couldn't go up to my parents, as I'd told them I was ill. To my side was a table I'd not noticed before, laden with food. That was odd. We never usually provided refreshments. I spotted a square of cheese on a stick, grabbed it and threw. The cheddar hit Dylan Thomas on the nose and he turned and looked at me haughtily. Without moving his eyes from mine he leant down to my mother's cheek and, slowly, deliberately, licked it.

That's when I lost control. 'Get off her, you animal!' I shrieked as I lunged towards the ghost. Moving with remarkable fluidity, Dylan Thomas slipped across into Susan's lap. I grabbed the jug from the podium, thought for a second, decided that I didn't mind soaking Susan at all, and emptied the water all over them both. There was a very gratifying scream from Susan but Dylan Thomas had moved on to the refreshments table and was tossing sausage rolls and vol-au-vents into the air with manic abandon. Now and again, he'd pause to stuff an egg sandwich into his mouth. The crowd gave way to panic. Those hit by food were trying to escape, trampling the people in the rows further back. Dylan found the Welsh cakes and stood on the stage, throwing them as if they were flat stones he was bouncing on a lake. I grabbed his legs, to pull him off stage, but my hands slithered on his shell-suit bottoms, which came off. He stepped out of them and ran around in Y-fronts, overturning chairs and sticking his tongue out lasciviously at female members of the audience. I saw him approach Peter and raise his fist.

I didn't know I could do a rugby tackle, but I'm not Welsh for nothing. Dylan Thomas saw me coming and made for the fire exit. With an instinct born of years of having to watch men in shorts wrestle each other into mud, I dived for his lower legs. I brought Dylan down in one devastating move. Then I sat on him.

He laughed in my face and did something I hope you never have to experience yourself. He possessed me. Imagine your body is a toasty sleeping bag and, in the middle of the night, a cold, damp shadow slips into it to be with you. Or you're wearing a wetsuit and instead of that thin layer of water between you and the neoprene keeping you warm, your skin explodes into a rash of poison ivy, rubbed raw on every surface. Or you're in a small boat and you're managing, just, to make your way across a choppy river until you take on board a person intent on standing up, so that your vessel rocks madly back and forth and you both topple into the water. Now that my mind was melded with Dylan Thomas's I saw chasms and crevasses of despair which horrified me and for the first time, I became fearful for my eternal soul.

That night, we decided to call in the exorcist. My feet were still hurting from the Abba boots, so I rode gratefully in the back of the car as my parents drove home. They still couldn't believe what they'd seen: objects and food flying around and no visible entity doing the throwing. Later I sat with them in the lounge as they aired their worst fears. They had heard strange movements around the house, knockings and snatches of voices from my room, sounds which disappeared as soon as they went to check. Things had gone missing from my father's study, papers and pens. And someone, my mother swore, had been stealing food.

First thing in the morning, they called Father Devonald. Yes, he could come later that day for a cup of tea. I watched from upstairs as my father answered the door and let in the priest. I then crept downstairs and watched them through the frosted glass of the lounge door. Father Devonald's deep voice droned on, underneath the higher, more nervous tones of my parents.

I found myself feeling agitated. For weeks I'd been struggling to come to terms with the increasingly bizarre events in my life. Now it had become too much. As I sat on the bottom stair I began to rock back and forth. I lifted my father's walking stick out of the hatstand and began to knock it against the wall. I was finding the repetitive sound soothing. I couldn't quite catch my breath, I could hear myself gasping. I leant into my parents' coats, took solace from smell. My forehead pressed through into the wall and I began to hit it, as a way of distracting me from my inner turmoil. One part of me stood aside and told myself: 'Don't worry. This isn't as freaky as it looks. You're having a panic attack.'

The lounge door opened and I heard a deep voice say to me: 'You're welcome to join us. Please come in.' I couldn't resist the invitation and made my way into the room, but I couldn't look anyone in the eye. I sidled past the back of the sofa and leant against the grandfather clock. I opened the door and began to play with the pendulum. This made the clock chime chaotically. I glanced at my parents. They were holding hands with the priest and his eyes were closed in prayer. I made a silent plea for him to rid me of Dylan.

Inside me, he was in such agony, that he had to do something to soothe the pain. Oh no, I thought, as he made me look at the mantelpiece with my mother's favourite ornaments. The brass candlesticks bounced but the Capo de Monte figurine didn't. Father Devonald and my parents jumped as I threw the Staffordshire dogs. I looked around

wildly, hyperventilating, and opened the corner cupboard. I
was aware that I was behaving like a rock star smashing up a
room, but I found the sound of objects breaking soothing.
Even when the cupboard itself crashed down, the three adults
carried on with their prayers. Eventually there was no more
furniture to overturn and the broken stuff settled – the
sideboard door squealing back and forth – I found strange
comfort in my mother's tears.

12

I decided to spend my first day free of Dylan Thomas down at the shack. I watched Swansea families spring-cleaning, their strimmers coughing to life, and soon the smell of cut grass made me feel homesick in a way I didn't understand. I *was* home, wasn't I?

I made my way down to the hollow where a fire burned in front of Julian's rambling (and almost certainly illegal) hut. Here they had professional amounts of firewood stacked under mouldy tarpaulins. Two children of indefinable sex ran in and out of the compound and from time to time miscellaneous adults emerged from the cabin, squinting in the light.

I settled myself on a log by the side of the fire. Smoke burned my eyes and I realised why everybody else was sitting upwind, but I felt so apathetic that I didn't move. Softly, almost without my noticing, Julian, dressed in a dirty sheepskin waistcoat, began drumming. I found the rhythm so comforting that I was surprised when the shadows had grown long and the sun began sinking behind the valley's trees. As I walked back to 'Fern Hill', the smell of cooking from the shacks already lit in the dark made me feel even more bereft.

I opened the door to find a meal of tinned salmon and salad laid out neatly on a table cloth. Dylan Thomas, wearing a cravat, held a napkin over his wrist and bowed. For a ghost who should have been driven from the face of the earth, he looked anything but ethereal. As I became more ennervated by the week's events, Dylan was, if anything, more invigorated... younger. The hair on his receding hairline seemed to have grown back and he'd lost the weight dissolute living had added to his frame. My God, he looked *healthy*.

He pulled out a chair for me to sit on and poured a light white wine into two mugs. I looked at him, suspicious.

'How did you manage to survive last night's exorcism?'

'Easy. I simply retreated into being my books for a while, so the priest had nothing to grab hold of. You can't get rid of writing as easily as you can a person. Mayonnaise, my dear?'

'Why do I get the feeling you want something?'

'I've had an idea. No wonder I'm suffering from writers' block. I need to go back to when I was at the peak of my powers, to the glory days in New York.'

'Isn't that what killed you?'

'But I'm older and wiser now. Besides, I'd have a chaperone, wouldn't I?'

When flying transatlantic with a ghost, do you book one seat or two? I've heard of musicians having to pay for their cello or guitar but, given that Dylan Thomas wasn't real, I wasn't prepared to pay for him. If push came to shove, he could always possess me and we'd take up less room. As luck would have it, our flight wasn't full, so we were both able to stretch out in rows of seats at the centre of a Boeing 747.

Things went smoothly until the drinks trolley came round. I went for a stroll but came back to find Dylan Thomas clutching a handful of miniatures to his chest. I kept an eye on him as the film began, but was increasingly worried by his rapid consumption of shorts.

'Go easy on those', I hissed. 'I don't know the effect of alcohol on a spirit.'

'I didn't tell you that I'm terrified of flying,' said Dylan Thomas.

'You're dead. You can't be afraid of anything. The worst has already happened to you.'

'That's what you think.'

'Besides, didn't you used to fly when you were alive?'

'In those days, we usually went by ship to America. Far more civilised than being penned into a tube like this.'

The truth was that Dylan Thomas had the boredom threshold of a two-year-old. I watched him warily as he fiddled and fidgeted in his seat. He seemed not the slightest bit interested in the film. He read the in-flight magazine then tossed it over his shoulder. He walked the aisles, staring shamelessly at our fellow passengers. I was just dropping off to sleep when I heard him shout: 'Hey! Jennie! There's a man here reading a book about me! How about that? Forty years dead and I'm still news!'

I raised myself in my seat to see Dylan Thomas leaning over the shoulder of a businessman.

I hissed as quietly as I could: 'Leave the man alone!'

'It's Caitlin! She wrote a book about me!'

'You're so vain! She wrote a book about herself and you're only part of the story.'

'I wish this bloke would hurry up and finish reading, so that I can have a look what she said about me.'

'Grow up!'

I went to the WC and washed my face in the tiny sink. I felt terrible, a hundred years old. My face was ashen. When I passed him on the way back, Dylan Thomas was blowing in the businessman's ear, trying to distract him. I put on the eye mask, reclined my seat and, soothed by the thought of Iceland passing below the plane, fell fast asleep.

I was jolted awake by a passenger announcement asking, urgently, for all passengers to return to their seats. Air hostesses were rushing around in a controlled panic. Instinctively, I looked round for Dylan but he was nowhere in sight. Instead, the flight attendant was in a tussle with the businessman who seemed to be trying to open the aircraft door. I realised that Dylan had possessed the poor man and was using his body. I sank down and hid in my seat. A steward rushed from the first-class section of the plane and joined in the struggle. The businessman was screaming that he needed to get out. His arms flailed as the steward sat on him. Suddenly all the fight seemed to go out of him and I watched as he was dragged past me, hands fastened with cable ties, to be locked in the rear WC.

Next thing, the plane lurched and took a sudden dive. The Fasten Seatbelt signs pinged repeatedly and the Captain's voice came over the tannoy requesting flight crew assistance in the cockpit. All the while the jet engines screeched and the terrified passengers held on to their armrests, thinking about death. Clearly Dylan was now fancying himself as an airline pilot.

What would I do if I knew I had only minutes to live? I could think of nothing that I regretted except that I hadn't told Peter how I felt about him. I certainly didn't want to be wasting my time with a dead poet on the rampage.

A few seconds later, the aircraft levelled out and Dylan Thomas came running down the aisle from the front of the plane. I began to think that we might not die after all. Looking around in case anybody saw me talking to myself, I pulled Dylan into the seat next to me and demanded to know what he'd been doing. I'd never seen him so agitated. He didn't answer my question but said in a desperate tone of voice, 'I've got to get off and see her.' I told him to calm down but he was beyond reason.

'I tried the emergency door but that wimp wasn't strong enough. So I dumped him. And that pilot, he's so rational I couldn't gain entry for any length of time. I tried to make him turn the plane round. I need to go back home right *now*.'

'But we're more than half way over the Atlantic!'

'I've got to see Caitlin.'

He started to cry like a child.

'But Dylan, Caitlin's dead.'

'She can't be. I don't believe you.'

'She's buried in the same grave as you. How could you not know?'

Dylan Thomas wailed. I could tell by their physical reaction that the passengers could now hear him. Their eyes became round with terror. I tried to calm him by recounting what facts I knew: 'Caitlin married again and had another child by an Italian. She was all right.'

This made him worse.

'I don't want her to be all right without me. She was *my* Caitlin. I should have gone back to her and now it's too late.'

He grieved to the bottom of his breath, bitterly, and the air went cold around us. Everyone sobered at the sound of such sorrow that it gripped us all from the other side of life. We think we grieve for the dead and that is unbearable enough, but while the living weep for individuals lost, the dead mourn for a whole word lost and feel the despair of being unable to change for ever. I put my arms around Dylan Thomas but there are some sorrows that even the most willing heart can't reach. The poet, wild with regret, began to wail.

13

I woke up to find Dylan lying next to me in a king-sized bed. I groaned inwardly. Surely not. I felt sorry for him, but not enough to… Gingerly I felt my nether regions in order to establish my state of undress. Yes, there were underpants and no they weren't damp. Perhaps we hadn't, after all. What a relief. I looked past Dylan Thomas's profile and was surprised to see the businessman sleeping sweetly in an adjacent bed. Then it all came back to me.

We were in Gander on the northeastern tip of Newfoundland. In the middle of Dylan's unworldly keening in the cabin the Captain announced over the sound system: 'Ladies and Gentlemen, this airline operates a zero tolerance approach towards alcohol abuse. Due to an incident involving a passenger, and in the interest of safety, this plane will divert to the nearest airport.' Knocking was heard from the businessman in the WC, but nobody moved to release him. Several passengers crossed themselves as the plane's wheels touched down on Canadian soil.

Once we reached the terminal at Gander, the businessman – still wearing a cable tie around his wrists – was escorted off the plane. Dylan Thomas insisted that I followed closely on his heels. He wanted to finish Caitlin's book, and it had to be *now*. The authorities must, eventually, have believed the man's protestations that he was both sane and sober, but I couldn't recall how he now appeared to be in our party.

I lay in bed, overwhelmed by the mess in which we found ourselves. Dylan was awake but trying not to be. I whispered viciously: 'All you had to do was behave, but no. It was too much to ask. If you hadn't messed this up, we'd be in New York now and I'd be closer to getting rid of you.'

'She said she'd never had an orgasm with me,' whispered Dylan Thomas. So that's what he'd seen in Caitlin's book. A tear trickled from the corner of his eye into his ear.

'I thought that I was her life. But she was mocking me.'

I tried to think of something encouraging to say. 'You've not been forgotten. But life goes on…' My voice petered out. 'Look on the bright side – "'Tis better to have loved and lost…"'

'Don't give me that crock of shit,' he replied bitterly and I fell silent.

The businessman moaned and began to stir. He ignored us both, leapt out of bed and went into the bathroom. While he was showering, I found his passport and learned that his name was Gordon. When he came out, Gordon continued the silent treatment. Soon, he picked up the phone to talk to his wife.

'Honest, Lind, I don't know what happened. One moment I was fine and next thing, I was trying to claw my way out of the aircraft. Like I was on acid… No, of course I don't know what that's like, but it's how I imagine… No, I wasn't drunk, I swear to you. I've a mind to sue them. And now they won't let me fly… I'll think of something.'

We followed Gordon down to breakfast and sat in silence. In all the rush, I'd left my handbag on the plane, but Gordon kindly picked up the tab, before leaving me and Dylan Thomas in the deserted diner.

'Did you know,' I said, reading from a card on the table, 'that Gander used to be one of the refuelling stops for transatlantic flights? And that the streets are named after famous aviators?' Dylan Thomas showed no interest at all.

'I can't bear to think of the terrible mess I left for Caitlin. If I could see her once to beg for forgiveness...'

'I'm sure she knows how sorry you are. After all, you and she were soulmates.'

'What good is a soul mate if all he does is make you suffer? She needed someone reliable and I never was. She deserved a much better husband, one who could provide for her and the children. She was right. *She* was always the catch, not me.'

Dylan Thomas crossed his arms on the table and put his head down on the table in despair.

What do you do if you're stranded hundreds of miles from where you want to be, with no money, no documents and a travelling companion who's dead? We checked all our pockets and turned out one glove, some small change, a boiled sweet and a length of string. We decided to hitchhike.

First we walked to the edge of Gander. Dylan had lapsed into a deep apathy from which nothing could shake him. 'This town's so old-fashioned,' I observed. 'It's forty years behind the times. Should suit you just fine.' I left him to sit in a heap at the kerb while I concentrated on thumbing, but no matter how winsomely I practised my 'we-won't-rob-you' smile, no one stopped to give us a ride. So we started to walk westwards.

On the outskirts of town, we reached a field from which a funfair was in the process of moving. 'I know!' I said, pulling an entirely apathetic Dylan Thomas along by the hand, 'let's run away with the carnival! I've always wanted to know what being a carnie is like. And Mam would never even let me go on the rides. I've got to do this before I die!'

Dylan Thomas trailed behind me as I wandered around the various rides watching the hands packing their vehicles. I'd taken a liking to Charlie, the Astroliner operator and hitched a lift for us both in his truck. Mercifully, Charlie was taciturn for reasons of his own involving a woman in a bar, so he talked little and played Country and Western ballads all day. All three of us listened to the lyrics and nursed our respective broken hearts. That night, Dylan Thomas and I slept platonically in the three-quarters bed in the back of the truck. Charlie drove in the dark to our next destination. Dylan Thomas was so miserable that I had no fears for my sexual safety. Great, I was travelling with one of the great love poets of the twentieth century and he didn't even fancy me. I didn't want him to, but it was the principle of the thing. I would have liked the chance to reject him.

When I got up in the morning, Dylan Thomas pulled the covers back over his head and refused to move. I walked around the midway, watching the carnies set up their rides. Already young girls had come in small groups to giggle at the men, who hammered metal bars into place, knowing exactly how lewd to be to make sure that the girls would return that night, half terrified, half entranced by their roughness.

I don't know why funfairs have the name of being happy places. As far as I could see, the carnies were a discontented lot. A young boy called Ray had adopted a dog two towns ago in order to guard his ride but the creature had never been heard to make a noise. He'd found out that the dog was a barkless breed so, instead of feeding the animal, he was throwing stones to drive it away.

It was evening by the time Dylan Thomas appeared. Whereas the field had looked messy during the day, night was forgiving. Electric light bulbs and music covered over the tackiness and gave the rides glamour. The poet slouched his way over to me, hands deep in his pockets. I asked: 'How are you, my friend?'

'I've not been a very good friend to you. If only you knew…'

'Course you have. You're just having a hard time at the moment, you're feeling low.'

'You wouldn't say that if you knew what I should have been doing instead of running round thinking only of myself. You should ditch me.'

'Don't you know that the best way to get a woman to stick with you is to warn her off you? Works every time.'

'I owe you a huge apology. You're not going to like it when I tell you…'

'Now, now. You've had a shock. You're being too hard on yourself.'

Dylan Thomas traced lines in the dust with the tip of his shoe: 'We shouldn't be here.'

'Well, I must admit that getting thrown off the plane wasn't part of the plan. But, hey, this is an adventure! Charlie's showing me how to operate the Astroliner.'

'You're being so nice, it makes me feel worse. I'm such a coward.'

'No need to feel bad at all. How many women get to travel with Dylan Thomas? Come on, let's go and get a hot dog. I'm starving.'

I'd hit the jackpot. Despite his uncharacteristic desire for self-flagellation, the promise of some cheap calories and mustard sauce – not to mention fried onions – brought a smile to Dylan Thomas's face and a spring to his step. By the time we were wiping the ketchup off our cheeks, we were the best of friends again and Dylan Thomas was pestering me for tickets to go on the rides. I'd found a book of them in Charlie's cab, so I handed half of them over. I smiled to see him ride the dodgems and the waltzers, as if living out his own poems.

But the melancholy that had dulled Dylan Thomas earlier had now infected me and I couldn't shake it. I took a few rides but soon felt sick and so contented myself watching the townspeople buying their way into a fantasy of motion and fear. I followed one family in particular. The father wanted to take his daughter into the Circle of Death. It was a tubular wall with handholds around the edge. The idea was that, as it spun round, the centrifugal force flung you hard against the side, so you were pressed down, quite safe, without having to hang on at all. The daughter – aged about twelve – wanted to join in, but her mother flatly refused to let her go. The girl had to stand with her mother, watching her father alone on the ride.

I had drifted close to them, in order to eavesdrop on the row, so I had a good view of the daughter's face as she watched her father spinning around. As it went round faster and faster, the circle tilted so that we could see in. Suddenly the girl's envy turned to terror as she saw her father as if he were dead. He was there but he could no longer see them. To him they were no longer people but streamers, abstract shapes among many points of light. And now he was pressed down by the terrible weight of speed, struggling with all his strength to bear it. The girl cried out but he couldn't hear her. And no matter what her parents said, even when her father, his knees shaky, came down off the ride smiling, she would not be comforted. I felt a breath on my neck and turned to find Dylan Thomas standing at my side: '*Now* do you see?' he asked.

What you don't realise about a funfair is that the carnies are always leaving. New faces arrived, attracted by the lure of easy come and easy go, the fair a body whose cells were dying and being replaced. One morning, one of the faces with whom we'd been drinking at the campsite the night before would be gone. On impulse, a man would take umbrage at something, or be reminded of more urgent personal business, leaving the remaining hands to sort through a small pile of belongings.

These usually consisted of some well worn t-shirts, maybe a sleeping bag and a pile of endlessly circulating Louis L'Amour paperbacks.

Dylan and I settled into a routine. I stayed with Charlie on the Astroliner, a fake rocket ride. Truth was, I'd fallen a little in love with Charlie. He was lithe and brown, with a Texan drawl. Our relationship had become pleasingly erotic. I spent hours tracing the contours of his muscles. He never seemed to mind how much I talked but he rarely felt the need to reply. I found such a total acceptance sweet and had begun to avoid Dylan Thomas and his moods. He worked the Ferris Wheel. Typical poet, once he got his hands on the microphone, he was never off it, calling the punters to come and ride. When he got bored, he shared his thoughts about life, his memories of his boyhood and, on one especially slow day, he gave a masterclass on the work of John Donne and the influence of the Welsh on the Metaphysical poets. I'm pretty sure that only I could hear his speeches, but I did notice that when he was on form and argued how a Ferris Wheel ride would produce the deregulation of all the senses so beloved of his mentor Rimbaud, crowds stood in line, as if they perceived his rhetoric on a sub-audible wavelength that they understood but couldn't hear.

One evening, Dylan Thomas came up to me in the town campsite where we'd pitched our tent. I was pushing myself lazily on one of the swings. I asked what was up.

'We've got to leave soon,' he said. 'Time's running out.'

'But I like it here,' I replied. 'This lifestyle suits me. Outdoors. Giving people pleasure. Much better than working in an office.'

Dylan Thomas was chewing on a straw. Come to think of it, I hadn't seen him smoke a cigar in a while.

'But we've got to move on.'

'What's time to you? Once you're dead you're dead.'

A suntan suited him and he looked healthier than usual.

'No, there's a certain window of opportunity and ours won't stay open for long. We need to get to New York.'

'Can't we just change the plan?'

'We had a deal.'

He dropped to the ground and did some squat jumps. A sleeveless vest showed biceps and triceps toned by heavy lifting.

I asked, 'Don't you like it here?'

'I don't mind it, but I'm thinking of you...'

'No you're not, you never do. You just can't stand seeing me happy for once with Charlie.'

'What about Peter? Or have your forgotten him? I thought that he was the love of your life.'

'Who said that a person can't love two men at the same time? I have a capacious heart. What about

"Not for the proud man apart
From the raging moon I write...
But for the lovers, their arms
Round the griefs of the ages."?'

'God you're so annoying. Look, I *know* that it seems to you as if we have all the time in the world, but we don't. Things will have settled into their fate very soon and if you want to change it...'

'You're just mean. I never had a chance to travel like you and now I've a taste of the open road, you want to hem me in. You're worse than my mother.'

'You'll thank me for this when you understand.'

'Blah, blah, blah. You even talk like her. I'm not listening.'

'It's for your own good.'

'What are you? Auntie Dylan? You've turned into a bleating old woman.'

'Just doing my job.'

'I thought it was me looking after you.'

'We need to talk about that.'

'So, if I'm in charge, I say we stay with the fair for the rest of the season and live a bit, for a change.'

'Right, you've left me no choice. If you don't come with me tomorrow, I'll make sure that a mysterious mechanical fault develops on the Astroliner at exactly the time when Charlie's magnificent body is under it inspecting the rig.'

'You wouldn't.'

'I would. Do you want to take the risk? We're still in Canada. If we don't make it down to New York and find out what's keeping me with the living dead, I know you'll regret it.'

'You've had your life. I haven't been anywhere or seen anything...'

'Would you come if I said we could make the odd detour?'

I thought for a moment. 'Niagara Falls. I've always wanted to see Niagara Falls. Almost as much as I've wanted to go to the top of the Empire State Building in New York.'

'Any reason for that?'

'Didn't you see *Sleepless in Seattle*? The last scene, when Meg Ryan meets Tom Hanks on the observation platform?' Dylan Thomas looked blank. 'What am I saying? Of course, you haven't seen the film. You probably died before they invented films.'

'Don't be cheeky. All right. We can take a detour very quickly to see the falls.'

'And I want to go in the boat – what's it called?'

'*Maid of the Mist*?'

'Yes, the full tour. Do you promise?'

And so, like so many other drifters attracted by the carnival for a while, we left without warning the following morning. I had nothing to give Charlie but a small teddy bear I'd won on the shooting range. I kissed him as he slept and Dylan Thomas and I turned south.

14

The real nightmare began when I spotted an Edgar Allen Poe lookalike skulking in a waterproof. The spray from the waterfalls had pasted his sparse hair in strands on the great dome of his forehead.

'Look! It's Edgar Allen Poe,' said Dylan Thomas cheerily. 'I haven't seen him in ages. He's really very sweet once you get to know him.'

'How can he be here?'

'Well, it's not so much him who's here but the poor sod who's with him.'

I took a second look and, sure enough, squeezed next to him on the bench facing the falls was a young man wearing a matching coat and clutching a plastic bag to his chest.

'Who's he?' I asked, but Dylan Thomas said he didn't know. Curious, I edged closer and when the *Maid of the Mist* turned midstream, most of the tourists moved for the view. I sat next to the man. Poe was still on his other side.

'So, how's it going?'

He looked at me and sighed. 'Could be worse, I suppose. Who's yours?'

Edgar Allen Poe gathered the long strands of his hair from his comb-over and tied them back with a fetching red spotted kerchief. I noticed his fingernails were long and dirty.

'Looks like Dylan Thomas, but healthier. That must be fun,' my new friend persisted.

'He's a bit of a pain, to tell you the truth.'

'Poetry's a terrible bore. Like crocheting. I'm Harvey,' and he offered me his hand, which was cold.

'Jennie. Pleased to meet you.'

Harvey opened the guidebook. 'Says here that the word "Niagara" is derived from the Iroquois Indian word "Ongniaahra", meaning "the strait".' I said nothing, so Harvey continued: 'Very suitable for an international and spiritual boundary. What's he like?'

The skipper of the *Maid of the Mist* turned the boat again, causing the tourists to gasp as a strong downdraught created by the falling water covered them in spray.

Dylan Thomas had turned my whole life upside down, but faced with Team Edgar Allen Poe, I felt strangely protective towards *my* ghost. 'He's growing on me. Seems to be getting younger all the time. Better behaved. More handsome.'

'Yes, it's funny that, isn't it? Who's he talking to now?'

I followed the direction of Harvey's stare. 'Can't quite see.'

Dylan Thomas suddenly roared with laughter. The stocky man standing next to him wasn't wearing a coat at all, and his bald head shone with moisture.

'That's Picasso,' said Edgar Allen Poe bitterly. 'Bloody charlatan.'

'What is this? A cruise for dead artists?'

'It's the way the water falls from the cliff of dolostone and shale. This uniting of two different levels of earth by water, the marriage of variation in a rainbow…'

'Ed, you're getting fanciful,' interrupted Harvey.

'Have it your way,' said Poe listlessly.

Harvey turned to me and whispered, 'I think he's depressed.

He's got nothing positive to say. It's moan, moan, moan. I mean, I find myself trying to cheer *him* up and that's not my job. Mind you, it could have been worse.'

'It could?'

Harvey nodded to the prow of the boat, where a tall figure was holding forth. The breeze carried snatches of a domineering voice saying something about Wisconsin glaciation. I heard the words 'lower Silurian' and 'Upper Ordovician' pronounced over a small man cowering in a turquoise poncho provided by the tour company. The listener looked as though he'd lost the will to live.

'That poor sod got Wordsworth.'

At that, the boat lurched and a warm rain fell across our faces. Edgar Allen Poe had been sick.

Dylan Thomas bounced up to me enthusiastically. The damp had made his hair curl into copper ringlets, which looked truly striking. 'What do you think?' he asked. 'One of the wonders of the world, or what?'

'It's great,' I answered. 'Only one snag. The whole boat seems to be full of ghosts.'

'You said it. These sites do attract the dead.'

'Like flies round a carcass?'

'It's something to do with the river being broken by the falls. It echoes what happens to you when you die. You carry on, but at a different level. People pick their own sites. The Victoria Falls are busy this time of year. But any waterfall has its complement of souls surrounding it. I think it's the tearing noise.'

The roar of the waterfall became oppressive, and I was tired, tired to death of shouting to make myself heard over the sound of the river, the boat engine and the oos and ahs of the soaking tourists. I looked to the top of the falls, trying to follow one drop of water down, down until it made me giddy. I turned to Dylan Thomas.

'It's time to stop messing about. We need to get on with the job we came here to do. Remember? You writing new stuff so that I can impress Peter and get on with my life?'

'Ah, I've been meaning to talk to you about that.'

My heart was filled with world-weariness.

'Look. Let's get to New York, sort out this wretched writing block, then get back to Swansea so that you can make Peter love me, like we agreed. Then we can both go our separate ways. I'm sick of the sight of you.'

Dylan Thomas had the sense not to say anything back. He just held my hand. Edgar Allen Poe was still retching into a bag. His companion rolled his eyes and, for the first time, I thought that being haunted by Dylan Thomas might not be so bad after all.

15

We took an overnight bus to New York, spreading our soaking clothes across the seat backs, where they steamed gently. The central heating was on so high that we slept the rest of the way in what had become, effectively, a sauna. I woke up briefly in the bright slanting dawn to see Dylan Thomas in his vest doing one-handed press-ups in the aisle.

'Where to now?' I asked, as we stretched our limbs in the Port Authority terminal. 'The 92nd St Y where they performed *Under Milk Wood* the first time? Or St Vincent's Hospital?'

Dylan Thomas looked confused. I reminded him, 'Where you died.'

'Ah. Yes. Thing is…'

'Now don't get vague on me. Which one is it? Can't you tell?'

'Now that we've reached New York, I suppose I've got to tell you…'

'Oh, I know. How stupid of me. Must be the White Horse pub in Greenwich Village, where you drank those eighteen whiskies.'

'Will you *listen* to me?'

'I know it must be painful for you to revisit these places, but the job has to be done.' I spoke briskly, like a nurse proposing an unpleasant procedure that needed to be endured if the patient was to get better. I pushed Dylan Thomas towards a subway map. 'You know the city, which line should we take?'

He studied the map. 'I don't know, I always took cabs.'

'Spoilt brat!' I muttered under my breath. I was getting impatient. We were so near to the end of our journey that I'd begun to fantasise about life without Dylan Thomas. His little-boy-lost act was becoming seriously wearing. I made an executive decision. We'd walk. The grid layout of Manhattan streets would make the journey straightforward. 'Come on!' I said in my briskest tone, 'Step out and we'll soon be there!'

Dylan Thomas protested again but I shooed him up the subway stairs into the late afternoon: 'No time for nerves!'

Dylan Thomas and I walked in silence. I tried to concentrate on one thing, reaching our goal, but as we made our way across town, I became entranced by the streets. Yellow cabs moved like wasps, darting in and out of the traffic. Subway manhole covers vented steam. I felt like I was in a film. I was Meg Ryan rushing through the city streets to meet Tom Hanks at the top of the Empire State Building.

We turned a corner and suddenly there it was, with its art deco spire touching the sky. It looked so familiar and yet so much taller than I'd imagined that I stopped in my tracks. 'Don't look up, like a tourist, or we'll be mugged!' chided Dylan Thomas. I looked at my watch. Four thirty. Around us bustled men and women in suits. If we were quick we could pop straight up and then make it to Greenwich Village for early evening drinks, the perfect Dylan Thomas *mise en scène*. They probably had an express lift to the top. It was just a small detour. It would save coming back.

Dylan Thomas complained, of course, but he admitted that he'd never been to the top of the Empire State.

'Too busy raising hell, I suppose, to see the sights.' I told him the plot of *Sleepless in Seattle* and how the Meg Ryan character had watched *An Affair to Remember*, where Cary Grant and Deborah Kerr agreed to meet at the top of the Empire State. Dylan Thomas looked blank. 'Must have been made after I...'

The wind hit us like a wall as we emerged onto the platform's stage. Half afraid of falling, I edged to the balcony and took a peek down. Beneath us the streets of Midtown Manhattan moved with a glittering, abstract beauty that was almost inhuman. I peered down and could see tiny heads below, so vulnerable compared to the polished metal and glass of up high that I felt an unexpected tenderness.

'A penny for them,' said Dylan Thomas, as we both stared out.

'I was just thinking how I've always wanted to visit this place, how I'd hoped it would be with someone very special.'

'Be careful what you wish for,' said Dylan Thomas and I was about to ask him what he meant when a man inside a gorilla suit came around the corner towards us. King Kong. I waved to him and he came to join us. Dylan Thomas turned to the city below and addressed Manhattan in his most orotund voice:

Beauty is but a flower
Which wrinkles will devour;
Brightness falls from the air,
Queens have died young and fair,
Dust hath closed Helen's eye.
I am sick, I must die.

All three of us fell silent. Eighty-six floors below, the traffic sounded like a long breath exhaled. Looking out over the ziggurats and pyramids of the world's commercial and political might, it came to me that all these temples to man's power were no more than stones in a graveyard. I began to cry. King Kong stood so close to me that his hairy pelt warmed me. On my other side, Dylan Thomas placed an avuncular arm on my shoulder.

We came down on the last elevator from the top. 'Did you meet who you wanted?' asked the man in the elevator.

'Nah, not today,' the gorilla said, taking off his head. 'Dunno why, but I feel blue as hell. Time to go home and kick the cat.'

Back at street level, couples met for drinks in bars after work. Actors arrived backstage and stared at their own faces in mirrors. We passed Korean grocery stores with piles of fruit so perfect they looked plastic, buckets full of gerbera daisies and roses. As the street numbers dropped, the offices gave way to the galleries and boutiques of Lower Manhattan. Dylan Thomas had hit his stride. By 14th Street, I was out of breath.

'Stop a moment! I've got a stitch!'

'That'll teach you to be so bossy.'

'I just want to finish the job in hand.'

Dylan Thomas looked around him, distracted. 'This looks familiar,' he said. 'Ah, I know. Follow me!' And he charged off, making me run to keep up with him.

We opened the door of the White Horse Tavern and walked into noise and smoke. Dylan Thomas plunged into the crowd, shouting over his shoulder to me: 'What can I get you?' I suddenly felt overwhelmed by people, inexplicably shy.

'Please,' I said, 'we're not here to drink.'

'Oh, go on. One won't harm. While we do what we came for.'

'I just want to be out of here.'

'Don't be a spoilsport. It's been so long since I was here. Just one, for old time's sake.'

'Oh, all right. Make mine an orange juice.'

'I'll get you a bourbon, it will do you good, relax you.' And with that Dylan plunged into the scrum at the bar. I made my way past the small circular tables, the wide wooden bar with its mirrors and frieze of horses' heads, to the back of the pub and locked myself into the Ladies' bathroom. I put the lid down on the toilet and sat on it. I felt exhausted after our walk, close to the end of my tether. I had a feeling of unfocussed dread, loneliness so profound that the groups of people chatting in the pub might have been in another dimension. There was no way that they could ever include me.

Someone knocked on the door and I shouted 'Okay, okay! Give me a minute!' I consoled myself with the thought that my business with Dylan Thomas was nearly over. Once we'd sorted out his writing, I'd be free to start my campaign to get Peter. After all, the whole point of a poet, especially a love poet, was to help ordinary people understand their passions. Dylan could tell me how to operate according to the secret rules of the soul. He could help me get my man. With a renewed sense of purpose, I washed and dried my face.

Whoever was knocking on the door had gone by the time I felt calm enough to emerge from the Ladies. If anything, the hubbub in the bar was even louder. A gale of raunchy laughter rose from a long table against the wall. Many of the other drinkers looked in that direction, enjoying the sound of hilarity. There, in the middle of a gang of women, sat Dylan Thomas, holding forth. He reached a punchline and set off another gale of dirty female laughter. Catching my disapproving eye, he stood up, holding a glass and beckoned me over. As I sat down at the table, I noticed that all the women were wearing red hats.

'What's this?' I asked. Dylan Thomas leant over, barely able to hear me.

'Red Hat Society. For women over fifty. Makes them feel better about being old.'

And, sure enough, the woman next to me wore a scarlet fascinator in her curly hair. Next to her was a cocktail hat in crimson satin with a coquettish veil. Next to her a fire-engine red fedora, then a felt cap with an ostrich feather that stroked the mirror behind her as the wearer nodded. Every single one of the women seemed to be talking at the same time.

'How can they see you?' I asked. 'You're a ghost.'

'Look around you. This is the one night I can appear with nobody knowing.'

I turned and looked. There were pictures of Dylan Thomas everywhere on the tavern wall: the young Dylan wearing a cardigan with Caitlin, Dylan dishevelled in a suit, not long before he died, Dylan sitting at the White Horse bar. In fact, Dylan Thomas seemed to be everywhere you looked. There was Dylan Thomas coming in through the door, Dylan Thomas sitting on his own reading *The Village Voice*, another Dylan leaning into the flame of lighter being held ... by Dylan Thomas? What was going on?

My Dylan Thomas laughed. 'It's a Dylan Thomas lookalike night! Isn't that hilarious? My friends in the red hats didn't know when they reserved their table, but they've opened a book about who can kiss the most Dylan Thomases. My money's on her!' Dylan Thomas pointed to a large woman who was moving towards the bar with a purposeful glint in her eye.

'Oh, and here's your drink!'

'I don't want it. I'm worried. This doesn't feel right.'

'She's already kissed me, so I suppose I'm Dylan Thomas number one. Though I think that one over there looks more like me than anyone else,' continued Dylan, pointing to a man who had chosen to wear a suit and bow tie. 'I'd never win. I'm much more fit than I was when I died.'

Have you noticed how, when there's a group of people applying themselves to getting drunk there's moment when the noise in the room performs a sudden crescendo? It mimics the action of alcohol in the blood, the perceived acceleration of synapses firing combined with an actual blurring of edges, a slowing of the eye and limb? Well, that moment happened and the bar of the White Horse Tavern hummed with mirth and mischief, lifted an inch off the floor of reality. Except I alone couldn't feel it. I sank down, lower and lower into a well of sadness of desolation. No one took any notice of me. Dylan Thomas was so busy being kissed by women in lipstick and garish dresses, they formed a cloud around him.

I reached over and tapped Dylan Thomas's shoulder. 'This isn't why we came! I've got to get out of here!'

'Can't you hang on for a bit? I'm really enjoying this. Just one more drink.'

I exploded: 'You selfish bastard! You promised me that you'd use this trip to sort out your writing. And all you're doing is getting drunk.'

'Actually, I think you'll find,' Dylan Thomas breathed hard into my face, 'that I'm stone cold sober. I don't drink the night before a ra...'

'The night before what?' I asked. I sniffed his breath. Coffee. And, for the first time, it seemed to me, I looked properly at what my companion had become. Surrounded as we were by men who were imitating the romantic idea of the cursed Welsh bard, damned by his sensitive nature to drink and untimely death, I saw that my Dylan was slim and trim. There was no sign of puppy fat or drink-bloat about him. He was lean with the wiriness of ... I grasped for the right analogy. Yes, I had it! Of a long-distance runner.

Now, looking back at our trip, I recalled long periods of our time with the funfair when Dylan Thomas went missing. I was so preoccupied with helping Charlie that I hadn't taken notice, but now I knew what he'd been doing. I looked at his feet. Trainers. No wonder he'd nearly killed me on the walk here.

I accused him: 'You've been in training. This whole thing was just to get us here so that you can run.'

He didn't try to deny it. 'It's the Brooklyn Half Marathon. Starts at 7 am tomorrow in Prospect Park.'

'Unbelievable. You tricked me.'

'You can't do a full marathon from cold, you've got to work up to it.'

'Let's get this clear. So did you have any intention of sticking to our deal?'

'Yes, yes. Once I've proved to myself I can do the race.'

'I come all this way with you believing you were really going to help me get Peter, when all the time you were just doing what you wanted. No thought of me!'

'It's not like that.'

'Caitlin was right, you're a selfish sod.'

He placed his hand on my shoulder and I shrugged it off. 'Don't touch me. This whole trip has been all about you. I hate you.' I made to leave but Dylan Thomas blocked my path.

'Jennie, you've got the wrong end of the stick.'

'No, I'm only beginning to understand how selfish you are. You've used me.'

'Calm down. Let me get you a drink.'

'I don't want anything more from you. I've had it.' My hand went out and grabbed my glass and before I could stop myself, I'd flung a Jim Beam right into his face. His mouth made an o. For a moment we looked at each other, in a freeze-frame. Then life sprung into action again. He wiped his eyes and liquid dripped from his hair. The bar was so jolly by now that nobody seemed to have noticed our little drama. I ran for the door.

I was crying so hard that I didn't care where I went, or if I was mugged. I heard my name being called behind me but ignored it. I headed towards the river, crossed the Westside Highway. All I could think was to find a place to sit alone. I was only dimly aware of wandering into a waterside area, out onto a wooden pier. Soon I could hear water lapping under my feet. I sat down on the end of the jetty and sobbed till there was nothing more in me.

I wasn't surprised when I felt Dylan Thomas standing behind me. 'Go away,' I said, but without conviction.

'Jennie, you need to listen to me now. I've tried to tell you, but not hard enough.'

'All you had to do was to sort yourself out artistically. But no,' I said bitterly, 'you want to start a new career as a runner. For fuck's sake, isn't it time you accepted that you're finished?'

'Jennie, my darling…'

'Don't darling me. You've had your chance, now it's my turn. And I want Peter.'

'Oh, sweetheart, you've really got no idea, have you?'

'What are you talking about?'

'Remember the carnival parade? You as the Muse? Did it really not register?'

'Yes, I dressed up as Caitlin.'

'There was an accident.'

'What's that got to do with anything? I remember a bit of a bump. That bloody disco float with a dancing floor and six John Travoltas – very vulgar. It shunted us. I fell off. Hit my head but I got straight back up, I'm not a quitter.'

'No, Jennie, you never got up.'

'I did and continued with my dance.'

'You only think you did.' Dylan Thomas sat down beside me and took my hand. 'I blame myself. I was late arriving but you were so intent on carrying on as you were that it's been very difficult to get through to you.'

'I don't know what you mean.'

'I'm trying to help you see. Didn't you notice that things weren't exactly as normal?'

'Everything was fine until that Susan turned up.'

'But wasn't Peter a bit funny with you?'

'He's a poet, what do you expect? He's preoccupied.'

But even as I made excuses for Peter, a new possibility was forming in my mind. I tried to push it away, but the smallest incidents which had puzzled me at the time began to make sense in this unthinkable new context. I brazened it out. 'Besides,' I said defensively, 'Peter likes me because I give him space to think. He can't bear constant chatter.'

The truth was, Peter hadn't been paying much attention to anything I said to him for a while now. My mind recoiled from the implication.

'And your parents? Have they been behaving as normal?'

I scoffed. 'My parents are a law unto themselves.' But they had been going very easy on me for a while, in fact, my mother had been far too busy crying to nag me for ages. 'Mam's just depressed.'

'And why do you think that might be?'

Behind us, I heard stifled laughter and against the streetlights, I could see two figures making their way into the shadow of a ruined warehouse. My mind was racing. Peter had been odd, more introverted than usual. No, surely not...

'I've tried to do the right thing, as they recommend, to go at your pace, but really, there's no easy way to tell you, Jennie.'

And Charlie, taciturn Charlie, never seemed to talk to me directly. Even in bed, he never took the initiative...

'I thought you'd get it at the memorial reading...'

And why was travelling so easy? We went through immigration at the Canadian border without being asked for our papers once. Just as well, I'd left ours on the plane. But then, I couldn't remember packing any.

'Now I'm confused.' I rubbed my temples. I'm usually so organised. I must have done…'

The voices were closer now, two men. I began to get nervous. A shout, the sound of something being thrown, echoing along the pier. Panic made me turn on Dylan Thomas.

'It's all your fault. Everything's been weird since you showed up. Why couldn't you sort out your own stupid problems?'

'I should have been straight with you from the start.'

'No, you should have just kept away, picked somebody else to haunt.' I was furious now. 'I don't even like your sodding work.' But Dylan Thomas continued to talk in a low, gentle voice.

'I'm sorry I lied to you, Jennie, that I played along with what you believed. I thought it was for the best.'

I looked back over my shoulder and jumped to see the silhouettes of two men still moving towards us. Confessions could wait. We could be knifed. 'Let's get out of here now!' I jumped up, pulling Dylan Thomas to his feet. He resisted.

'Truth is, Jennie, they can't do anything to harm us. The can't even see us.'

'Speak for yourself!'

Next minute, the two men had passed and I saw them pause, outlined against the water. They weren't muggers but lovers and they stopped to kiss.

'They can't see *you*, but I'm still here,' I countered.

'Are you sure about that?' asked Dylan Thomas so softly that I knew that what I feared was true. A boat steamed past,

ADVANTAGES OF THE OLDER MAN

breaking up the oily reflections in the water. The wake slapped against the piles beneath us in the dark.

'If I were dead, I'd be the first to know,' I said, my voice thin with emotion.

'Not always the case. Oh, Jennie, I'm so, so sorry.'

I was trying to take it in. 'Are you telling me that I died but I never even felt it?' I thought they'd cut the parade rather short. Things *had* been strange at home. I considered the last few months. 'And that I was at my own memorial service?'

He nodded, mute.

The pain, when it came, made me double over. The poem. Peter had written me an elegy. To him, I was a corpse. But Susan, Susan could touch him whenever she wanted. Phone him, shout at him, buy him a drink. Make love to him. I could do none of those things, nor would I ever. For Peter I no longer existed. Now I was a nothing and Dylan Thomas had strung me along, made me hope, as if I were still alive...

'You *knew* I was dead and you didn't tell me?' I flinched with the shame of it. A whole vista of cruelty was opening up: 'You've been laughing at me.'

'No, no. Jennie, I promise.'

'Ah yes, I can see it now. Must have been very amusing. Let her think she's alive, see what she does. You've made a fool out of me. And all this time, I thought I was helping you and you let me believe it.'

'If I could have thought of a better way, I'd have done it, but you were in such denial.'

'So it's my fault now? That's rich. Seems to me that all you've been doing is pleasing yourself all along.'

'I should have explained about dying and how there's a certain amount of time to set a new course.'

'You've used me. Anything to get to New York.'

'No, Jennie. I can get to New York any time I like. Can't you see that this journey…'

'If I'm dead, then why do I have to spend time with you? Can't I be dead on my own?'

'All the stops on this trip have given you the chance to do things you always dreamed about. Things you needed to do before letting go. Think for a moment. Didn't you always want to operate a fairground ride?'

What he said was true. As a child I'd planned to run away with the fair that came every year on the Mumbles road. But I'd never told anyone that. He continued: 'Visit Niagara Falls?' He had me there, though I wouldn't admit it. 'And, Jennie, most important of all didn't you always want more than anything in this world to have a human relationship? To feel close to someone? To be understood?'

Now I was really angry, but rather than thinking of something smart to say I felt a lump in my throat and hot tears in my eyes.

'Jennie, my darling, you haven't lived, so how can you die?'

'How dare you? Who are you to say? You made a mess of everything. You ruined yourself.'

'Yes, but at least I loved and was loved in return. Can you say the same?'

I thought over the years of rented rooms in other people's houses. The solitary place laid for breakfast. My grey underwear in a bowl, soaking. I'd run away from people, used my routine as a way to avoid them. Sure, I'd had sex, but that had never mattered much. I'd never looked into somebody else's eyes with confidence, and known that they'd seen me. I hadn't been human and now it was all too late. My chance was gone.

Dylan Thomas sat down beside me, swung his legs over the water. 'I know you're in shock, but it's not all bad news.'

'What are you saying? That there's an up side to finding out I'm dead?' I laughed bitterly.

'That's why I'm here, we all have a chance. There's an in-between period when things can be changed in our internal fate. Not everyone gets the opportunity. I came especially for you.'

'You shouldn't have bothered.'

'Think of paintings of the resurrection. The people in hell are always alone, being tormented. But heaven's a party where the soul's a guest. We're meant to live our lives in company.'

'I've got to see Peter, it's him I love. He'll make me human.'

'No, Jennie, he's no use to you.'

'You're just jealous.'

'Jennie, I know you wouldn't have chosen me as a friend, but we're more alike than you might think.'

I scrambled to my feet and began to plan. First thing was to dump Dylan Thomas. I picked my way over the missing planks along the pier and towards the highway. Dylan was still talking as he followed me: 'One of the reasons we don't get on is that we're so much alike.'

I scanned the traffic for an available cab. Dylan Thomas pulled down my upheld arm and looked me full in the face. 'Don't you see the resemblance?' You remind me so much...'

'Leave me alone.'

A car honked its horn at us, changing its pitch as it passed. Dylan continued: 'You wouldn't believe how frightening the bombing was during the war. When you heard those incendiaries coming, terror made us all do things we wouldn't in peace.'

The traffic lights changed from red to green and cars began to accelerate towards us. 'Jennie, I've waited a long time for you.'

The poet stood on the Westside Highway and, with a look

of pity on his face, opened his arms to me and smiled so sweetly and so sadly that I nearly went to him in gratitude and relief and joy at finding, at last, a kind of home in the dark, confusing and discouraging world.

'You fucking pervert! Get away from me!'

I shoved him hard into the path of the oncoming traffic. I heard tyres screech. He'd be all right, he was already dead and I had unfinished business elsewhere.

16

What you don't realise until you're dead is that it's the living who haunt the deceased, not the other way round.

Of course, there was no need for planes and trains in order for me to travel. Now I understood that the whole pretence of flying transatlantic had been part of Dylan Thomas humouring me in my delusion that I was still alive. For the dead who know their condition, travel is merely a matter of will.

I chose to be in Owen's Field. One of Julian's raves was reaching its climax. Peter was there, dancing on his own in the light of a bonfire. He moved with the reckless abandon of the highly self-conscious who have, at last, let themselves go.

When you love somebody from afar, you know how hyper-aware you become of their body language? Of how long they stare at another woman? How you're so attuned to every nuance in the beloved's voice that you can see the workings of their heart, even if everything you've observed tells you the very thing you don't want to know: that they adore someone else? I brought that attentiveness to bear on Peter. I saw when someone slipped a tab into his drink, how he picked it up and drank from it, deep, thirsty from dancing.

I watched from the shadows as his eyes grew huge behind his glasses. Now he's started to sweat and seems to be staring at the flames in the bonfire. Soon, he's agitated, his arms moving as if sculpting light. Then he's running around, knocking into people. And I try to help him, but my arms won't hold him. I'm weaker than fog in sun, I can't reach him. He's climbing through brambles, when a clump of ivy catches his foot, sends him flying. He lies there, cold, looking up at the stars and I move like a black cat, curl up at his back. Then Susan comes, searches till she finds him, gently lifts him up, takes him by car to her flat. There, she wraps a blanket around him, plays gentle music, gives him a book of paintings to look at while his mind calms down and he sleeps. She does the work of the living.

Dawn's breaking when I swoop through suburban gardens, enter my parents' house to find my mother awake in front of the TV. My father enters and says: 'Come to bed, Eileen. You've watched that film enough.'

'It was her favourite.' On screen, Meg Ryan meets Tom Hanks and takes his hand. My father touches her shoulder and then she's crying. 'I should have told her who her grandfather was. And her visiting that Centre so often. There's no shame in it these days, not like during the war.'

I try to speak to them to tell her that I already know, but all I can manage is the sound of rain against the glass.

In despair I recoil and next thing the house is small and I enter the jet stream of souls that flow around the globe, restless as starlings of an evening. I try to find comfort in polar regions, where glaciers groan and calve ice, and the breath of whales is frozen in bubbles of air on the undersides of floes. Then I seek refuge in deserts so parched the sun's secret hunting song is heard by those dying of thirst. But I was already changed, so I make my way back to the only notion of home I have in my new condition.

Dylan Thomas is struggling on mile ten of the Brooklyn

Half Marathon. Although he'd been training as much as he could, he's lost touch with the group in whose corral he'd started out – it seems – hours ago. He's like a leaf that had been carried by the multicoloured stream of runners, a torrent at first, except now their numbers has thinned and so the force of the water is no longer strong enough to sweep him along. Even the crowds shouting encouragement along the route have given up on the stragglers.

I see him slow to a walk, clutching his side. Any second, he's going to sit down. I sneak up behind him and as he begins to fold I push the back of his knee with my own, then lift him back on his feet. 'Oh, no you don't. You have to go on.'

Dylan Thomas groans. 'Let me sit down, I'm in agony.' I drag him on, my arm round his waist.

'If you stop now, you'll never get up and where will that leave you for the marathon?'

'Don't. Care.' he gasped, 'Must. Been. Mad. Too Heavy. Not. Built. For this.'

Part of me enjoys seeing him suffer but now I've a vested interest in him making it to the finishing line. I try another tack. 'Come on, only a few miles to go, you've done the worst.'

He's staggering now, looking disoriented. 'What … you … know … 'bout … running?'

'Nothing, but you're so close. Please don't give up.'

His eyes were wild. 'No use. All in.'

I change my tone to one of derision. 'Just as I thought. You're all talk. What were you saying to me about making a new beginning? You haven't changed at all. You're just a dead poet. A Has-Been.' I trot ahead, not looking back. I hear him panting. 'Besides, I wouldn't want to be related to a man who failed to complete his first competitive race.' He's still making inarticulate noises, but I notice that they've resumed a rhythm. I sneak a look back. He's picked up his feet, lifted his head and is starting to jog again. I pick up my own pace and call over my shoulder: 'I'll beat you, Grandad!'

It's late when we cross the finishing line and the boardwalk is littered with discarded plastic cups. Dylan Thomas hobbles along, triumphant. The sun has gone down over the Long Island Sound, leaving a light without shadows, soft as absence of judgement. A tang of burnt sugar travels on sea air and I can hear snatches of bright music.

'What is this place?'

'Coney Island.'

'I wonder if they have an Astroliner.'

'You look younger already,' said Dylan Thomas and so did he.

Acknowledgements

I would like to thank Bernard Mitchell for allowing me to use selective details from his *A Virtual Dylan Thomas* project. I'd also like to thank the Dylan Thomas estate for permission to quote from 'In my craft or sullen art' and 'And death shall have no dominion'.

I'm very grateful to Penny Thomas for her meticulous editing and my agent James Macdonald Lockhart for his support.

Gwyneth Lewis has published eight books of poetry in Welsh and English, and was Wales's National Poet from 2005-6, the first writer to be given the Welsh laureateship. She also wrote the six-foot-high words for the front of Cardiff's Millennium Centre, rumoured to be the largest poem in the world.

Gwyneth Lewis's most recent collection, *The Sparrow Tree* (Bloodaxe 2011) won the Roland Mathias Poetry Award, and several of her previous poetry collections have won national awards. Her first non-fiction book *Sunbathing in the Rain: A Cheerful Book on Depression* (Harper Perennial 2002), was shortlisted for the Mind Book of the Year and her adaptation of the play for BBC Radio 4 won a Mental Health in the Media award. *The Meat Tree*, a version of the Blodeuwedd myth, was one of Seren's New Stories from the Mabinogion Series.